COCKY JOCK WOLF

BIG WOLF ON CAMPUS
BOOK ONE

AIDY AWARD

PIPER FOX

Paperback ISBN: 9781950228447
Audiobook ISBN: 9781666693102

Formatting by Kate Tilton's Author Services, LLC (www.katetilton.com)

COCKY JOCK WOLF

Nerdy, chubby girls don't date quarterbacks... or werewolves.

Eli:

I just want one night off of being the all-star golden boy that the entire world, including my pack, expects great things from.

Is it too much to ask to go watch my favorite horror movies and eat popcorn?

Apparently it is.

I just might get my chance if this cute AF nerdy book girl at the bar plays defense for me. As long as I don't let my wolf get a whiff of her ripe, delicious scent. The last thing I need to add onto my plate is a fated mate.

Charlize:

Go on a date or get fired - that's the ultimatum from my boss at the Moon Bean coffee shop. But I picked a real jerk and now I'm stuck at the bar with him.

I don't need anyone to save me, but a smart girl recognizes a good escape plan when she kisses one.

It's not like I'm going to fall for a jock with more notches on his belt than books on his shelf. But Eli is more than that and I'm developing some crazy feelings for him.

That is, until he turns into a werewolf straight out of a horror movie.

***Cocky Jock Wolf* is a fated mates New Adult paranormal romance with a nerdy, dirty, cute, and curvy girl and the captain of the football team (who is secretly a wolf shifter!)**

For everyone who ever fell in love with a cocky jock

"I love how in scary movies the person yells out 'hello?' As if the killer is going to be like 'Yeah, I'm in the kitchen. Want a sandwich?'"

— SOMEONE HILARIOUS ON THE INTERNET

ELI

One night. That's all I wanted. That's all I needed. Just one night under the new moon.

Not with a girl. That was easy. I'd racked up plenty of one-night stands. Came with the alpha wolf football star territory. I had a ball bunny knocking on my door most any evening, whether or not she knew I was a wolf shifter.

I was always down for some arm candy, or bed candy. The stream of cheerleaders, Bay State University Dire Wolves fans, and even a fresh out-of-school alum or two made me look like a sex god.

Lord knew my fucking life was all about what made me look good.

Good grades, great looks, stellar skills on and off the field. Being the best at everything got me what I wanted, prepared me to be the alpha of the Chincoteague pack someday.

Except tonight.

I just wanted one night off. Ten hours where I didn't

have to be the star, the jock, alpha heir to a pack, or the king of the campus.

Didn't look like that was going to happen. Because here I was at The Wolf's Den, everyone's favorite bar, celebrating the big win today with the entire offensive line. Again.

"Dude," Ty lifted his hand and gave me a stinging slap to the back, "when you threw that last pass, I couldn't even hear myself think over the fucking crowd going bonkers."

"School records are for pussies." Luka waved over the one and only female bartender.

"Whoo! Let's get our boy laid." Nik wrapped his arms around my shoulder. "You deserve a reward, man."

Kirill rubbed his hands together and scanned the room. "Game theory, guys. We hook Eli here up with the hottest chick and the rest of us get her friends."

Sigh. That wasn't even how game theory worked. But I would not be the nerd who corrected them. I let the guys scan the bar for chicks to pick up and ordered myself the Eli-Teagan-quarterback-special from the bar. Sparkling water, room temperature, with a twist. It was the season, and I was in training. No way I was fucking up my shot at going first round in the draft next year for a beer. I didn't need a scout seeing some TikTok video of me doing shots.

"Ew, get off me." The girl and her boyfriend standing next to me at the bar gave her guy a shove. He was clearly blitzed and didn't even notice when he bumped into me. My senses went on alert and my wolf rose up, seeking the danger.

Down, boy. It's just a bar, just a drunk guy, and just a girl who smells like ripe fucking peaches and moonlight.

"Come on," drunk guy swayed and grabbed the bar to stay upright. "I just want to make out, maybe grab a tit. It's not like I'm going to fuck you, you're fat."

Oh, Goddess. Yeah, buddy, that's the way to get a girl to let you kiss her and feel her up. What a douche.

"This was a mistake. I wouldn't kiss you if you were one of my book boyfriends come to life. I'm leaving. Who cares if I get fired?" The girl grabbed her bag and her book off the bar and slid from the barstool.

This dickhead was crazy. The girl had curves for days. Curves for miles. Curves I could get lost in.

"You're not going anywhere. I bought you a fucking expensive froo-froo drink. You owe me." The asshat grabbed curvy book girl's arm.

Oh, hell no. I may have a string of one-night stands notched into my headboard, but no girl owed me or any other guy a kiss or sex or even a fucking smile. My wolf was feeling overly protective of this cute and curvy nerd, too. "I don't think my girlfriend has anything for you except the finger, asshole."

I grabbed the douche by his shirt and shoved him into my offensive line. They had my back on and off the field. Plus, three out of the four of them were also wolf shifters like me and could fuck this guy up if I wanted them to. Not that revealing ourselves as anything other than your average elite college athlete was allowed.

"Hey, Eli. Eli Teagan. Fuck. You're Eli Teagan. I didn't know she was your girlfriend. I'm sorry, dude." In an instant, three six-foot five two-hundred and fifty plus pound grouchy-ass wolf shifter football players had this guy surrounded, leaving me to check on the girl.

I pivoted and nearly forgot how to talk, looking at how god-damned pretty she was. "Are you all right?"

She stared open-mouthed at the huddle, flicked her gaze up to mine, and then back again. She hugged her book and her bag to her chest, shook her head, and backed away. The bar was extra crowded because of the win, and she was going to have a hard time getting out of there through the throng of people.

I slapped one of my guys on the shoulder. "I'm gonna take this one for the team. See you guys later."

When I turned back to book girl, the daggers in her eyes were aimed straight at my heart. She held up a finger. "A. I don't need you to save me, and B. you're going to take one for the team? Really?"

Shit. "I didn't mean it like that."

Time to turn on the charm. I put on my best you-know-you-love me smile and flicked my gaze down to her lips and back up again. Chicks got all swoony for that move. I let just the tiniest edge of my wolf out, too. That made all the girls go wild. There was always something extra sexy about being chased by a predator.

When I leaned in to whisper in her ear, she was mesmerized and didn't move a muscle. I couldn't help a glance down at the pretty skin beneath the collar of her shirt. Exactly where a mate mark would go. "Look, just pretend for two minutes that we're together. We'll walk out that door like we can't keep our hands off of each other. I promise we can part ways in the parking lot. You'll get away from the douchehole and I'll get the night off I've been hoping for. You in?"

I'm sure to the rest of the bar it looked like I was whispering sweet nothings into her ear, charming my way into her pants. Not a single guy would cockblock me and I could finally get the hell out of here without anyone knowing where I was going, what I was doing, or breathing down my neck.

She glanced at the mass of people she was going to have to push through, and her shoulders sagged. "Fine."

Rock on. I put my arm around book girl's waist, and it took the damn will of a saint not to grab her plump ass. "Excuse me, people coming through."

The wall of people shifted and cleared a path for us. Book girl stared up at me like I was a freak of nature. Weird. That was not what I expected. All I could do was grin like a loon back at her. She wrinkled up her nose at me and damn if I didn't want to kiss that look right off her face. What the fuck was wrong with me that I needed her to like me right here, right now?

Book girl stepped out of my hold on her waist, and I had to bring out the moves to keep up. I slid my hand into the small of her back and guided her through the crowd. The second we were out the door, she slapped my hand away.

I was so wrapped up in this girl that I hadn't noticed the guys had followed up and brought the asshole with them. One of them actually picked the guy up and tossed him into the grass between the street and the parking lot.

He got up and wavered slightly, pointing to me and book girl.

Shit. He was about to call me out on the lie that she was my girlfriend. I could see it in his face, smell it in his scent. So, I did the only thing I could think of to save face. I kissed her.

*H*e kissed me. He flipping kissed me.

I'd really like to say that I slapped him silly. But I didn't. I. Kissed. Him. Back.

What the hell is wrong with me? Ugh.

For being super smart, I'm super dumb. First off, I should have known better than to go to The Wolves' Den on a Saturday night after a football game. That's normally the nights we close the coffee shop up early and I spend a nice quiet night in reading whatever newest release we've gotten in for merch sales that week.

Tonight's was a new sports romance from one of my fave authors. I wouldn't have even considered entering the devil's den of iniquities next door if Selena, the coffee shop owner, hadn't threatened my livelihood.

Now here I was making out with the Dire Wolves' star quarterback. I might choose books over balls, but I knew who Eli Teagan was. Everyone knew him. At least the name, anyway. I don't think I'd ever seen him in real life.

Just those enormous banners that hang from the athletic center.

He was actually a lot better looking in person, which was hard to do. I think half the girls enrolled at Bay State University probably masturbated to that particular image of our school's number one most eligible bachelor.

Not saying I had. I was more the Matthew Macfadyen as Darcy or Michael Fassbender as Rochester kind of girl. Romantic heroes did it for me, not jocks who didn't know better than to have sex in their socks.

Not that I knew or anything. The only jocks I'd ever slept with were the ones in romance novels when I fell asleep reading in bed.

My sense and my sensibility had clearly gone on a long walk through the moors, because I didn't even have the sense to break the kiss first. He was the one who pulled my tongue out of his mouth. When I blinked, we both kind of had that dazed what-the-hell-just-happened look. He rubbed his thumb over my lips and his voice was hot and husky. "Come on, let's get out of here."

"Okay." Was that really my voice, all breathy and whispery?

Geez. It was. Okay? Oh-kay? No. I was definitely not okay. I was not going home with a guy who had more notches on his headboard than books on his bookshelf. So why did I let him take my hand and drag me down the sidewalk that went between the bar and the coffee shop?

Maybe because Selena was right, and I was afraid of real life boys. Book boyfriends didn't break up with you and shatter your heart. Book boyfriends didn't tell you to lose weight, dress sexier, and hide your smarts. I never wanted to hear anything like that ever again. I had curves, liked to wear jeans and sweatshirts, and was here on an academic scholarship.

The thing was, I didn't give any guys a chance to be as good as a book boyfriend, because I never went out with any of them. But I did complain about them all being horrible jerks. Most of them probably were. But what if this one, this guy I had all the preconceived ideas about, wasn't a jerk?

I followed him down the sidewalk and into the alley behind the shops, hoping that I wasn't making a huge mistake.

As soon as we cleared the building, he pulled me to the side where no one would see and put his back against the wall. He took a long deep breath, closed his eyes, and lifted his face to the overcast sky. It was almost like he'd been trapped back there and could breathe now.

"Hey, are you okay?"

Eli blinked a few times and turned his head from side to side, stretching. "Yeah. Thanks for going along with that. I thought we were busted for sure. So, where you headed off to now? I'd offer you a ride, but I came with the guys."

Screech. That was my brain putting the brakes on every single one fantasy that had been running through my head. Once again, I was the smart girl who was also really dumb. I actually thought we were going to get out of there together. I thought he was going to take me back to his place and...

Dumb.

"I'm just gonna go home." That had been what I wanted to do tonight, anyway.

"Cool. You want me to walk you?" He looked at his watch.

"No. I live just across from campus. My car is right here. I don't like to walk home at night after I close the shop. Don't worry, I'll be fine." Geez, I sounded like an idiot.

He gave me the eye. You know, the one that says he can tell I'm being weird. "You sure?"

"Yeah. I'm sure." I waved him off. The sooner he left me alone, the sooner I could go die of embarrassment. "Go do whatever it is you wanted to do."

"Thanks. You're the best. The next time you need a fake boyfriend at the bar, let me know." He gave me a salute and jogged down the ally in the opposite direction of the bar. I sort of thought he'd go back in. Spread his exploits of making out with me in the ally.

Not like I was brag worthy for a guy like him. He probably had a cheerleader, or the captain of the cheer squad, waiting for him and that's what he was in such a hurry to go do.

I got into my car and started it up with every intention of going home. Really, I did. But I was too keyed up. This was a weird night and a cup of tea and a book just would not do it for me right now.

There had been that flyer for the all-night old-school horror movie festival at the coffee shop. I was totally that kind of nerd girl. Yeah, I liked romance and horror. The best horror movies had a little romance in them, anyway. Like that one old Michael Jackson Thriller video, where he turns into a werewolf and then a zombie on his date.

The old one-screen theater off campus was only a few blocks. It would be easy enough to take in the next show and gorge myself on popcorn and Dots.

I pulled into the parking lot and hurried up to the ticket booth. The 1954 classic *Creature from the Black Lagoon* was starting in six minutes. Perfect. The only other classic monster movie I loved better was the 1941 *Wolf Man*. The guy ahead of me got his ticket and turned to go into the theater.

"Book girl? What are you doing here?" Eli looked around like I was the paparazzi, and he was waiting for the rest of the cameras and screaming fans to pop out of the bushes and start tearing his clothes off. "Did you follow me?"

This guy was a wreck. Kind of cute that he thought of me as book girl and not make out in front of the bar girl. I'd give him one brownie point for that. But he was losing it right away for not learning my name. "It's Charley, short for Charlize, not book girl, and no. I came to see the movie. Monsters who fall in love with human women are my jam. You too?"

I pointed up to the board listing the show and times.

"Oh. Yeah, uh, me too." He looked down at the ground and kicked at an invisible pebble. And he blushed. Like actual, adorable, embarrassed, blushing.

You could have knocked me over with a feather. Hot jock guys like Eli Teagan had the ego of a tyrannosaurus rex. I doubted his vascular system even knew how to make him blush from lack of experience. It hit me right in the old noggin. He wasn't here with a bunch of his jock friends. In fact, he'd done everything he could to get away from them to come here.

Aww. He was an old-school horror nerd and didn't want any of his friends to know.

That seemed ridiculous to me. People were allowed to like more than one thing. But maybe not in his world. Jocks ate, drank, breathed, and lived sports, as far as I knew. Probably especially during their big season. To get to where he was, he probably lived football twenty-four seven since he was a kid. Didn't leave much time for geeking out over black and white horror movies or anything else.

I'd been miffed at him when he left me behind the bar, but now I kind of felt for him. It has to suck to not be allowed to be yourself. I straight up knew I was kind of weird, totally a dork, a geek about a lot of things, and I fangirled out all the time, especially about my favorite authors' new books, especially the paranormal romance ones. I was okay with who I was most of the time.

Other people weren't. Society wanted me to be taller, thinner, tanner, to eat more salad, and be interested exclusively in the reality TV shows like *The Bachelor* instead of Hitchcock's *The Birds*. I dealt with that by not being around society.

Didn't seem like Eli had that choice.

"That's cool. Looks like there are a lot of good ones on tonight for their festival. Gonna stay for a few?"

He looked up from the ground all dorky shy-like. "Yeah. I bought the all-night ticket. We missed *Nosferatu*, but *Invasion of the Body Snatchers* is on later."

He skipped right over *Wolf Man*. I lifted my hands in the air like claws and prepared to howl up at the sky. "Hey, don't forget my werewolf fantasy come to life. Ahroooo!"

Eli choke-laughed and joined me in my wolf-style cry. He did a spot-on imitation. Almost sounded real. After he was all smiles. He really did have a killer grin. "Come on, lemme buy you some popcorn."

He also insisted on buying my ticket, even when I told him not to. I wagged my finger and shook my head at him, but when he wasn't looking, I secretly smiled. He didn't need to know I liked he insisted on paying, like this was a date or something. I was gonna get my feminist card revoked for goodness' sake.

We took way too long arguing the virtues of Dots versus M&Ms in popcorn and the theater was already dark when we got in there. Eli held onto my elbow to lead me all the way to the back of the theater like he could freaking see in the dark. "Wait, let's sit in the middle of the middle. Everyone knows those are the best seats for the acoustics."

"Yeah, but the back is darker, better visuals."

I wouldn't win this battle. It's not like I hadn't seen this movie a hundred times and knew most of the dialogue line for line. To the back we went. The second we sat down, Eli manspread, like he was the king of the theater. Legs wide and arms over the back of the seats. One arm over the back of my seat.

If he pulled the yawn and try the cop-a-feel move, I was going to... probably let him. In fact, if he didn't do the move by the end of the opening credits, I might just do it to him.

Yeah, I know the best seats in the theater are smack dab in the middle. We were sitting in the back in the dark so I could hide the rocket about to explode in my pants.

Charley smelled so damn good, not just like the ripe peaches from before, but also old books, and licorice. Even if I stuck popcorn up my nose, I was never going to forget her scent. Man had it been a huge mistake to put my arm around her, because now I had to use my other hand to balance the bucket of popcorn on my lap. Every time she reached for a handful, my dick screamed that she should be reaching for me.

My wolf was going so crazy inside, wanting to kiss her and lick her and bite her and... claim her.

I was not ready to claim a mate. I had the pressure of a career in sports while not revealing my true self, the future of our pack, and Professor Rojo's literature in translation mid-term coming up. None of those gave me time to even consider a mate.

Besides, she was a human and while it was no longer forbidden to mate with them, it still felt hella taboo. Which of course, made her all the more delicious. Sure, most of us grew up dating the humans in the towns we lived in, but we couldn't ever reveal who we were to them.

Why was I dying to let her see the real me?

Just because she was the hottest thing since Hot Pockets, and was funny and into old horror movies, and did I mention how hot she was? She didn't even seem to notice either my hard on or how much I was drooling over her and all those curves. I was going to have wet dreams about that ass. She was so far from the typical girl I dated or even took home for a fling, I didn't know what to do with myself.

She didn't seem the type to be impressed by game stats or whatever. She was sweet and... bookish, and she kissed like a fucking siren. I hadn't been this nervous around a girl since I lost my virginity and even then, it wasn't like I had to work for it.

"Dot?" She held up the box of sticky sweet candies. I hated Dots, almost as much as Good n Plenties. Yuck.

"Sure." I took one and stuck in my mouth. Ugh. Cherry or some shit. It was like chewing cough syrup.

"Ah." She sounded disappointed. "You got my favorite flavor. There are never enough red dots."

Yes. I almost fist pumped the air. This was my in. "I'm happy to share."

I leaned in slow to make sure she was down for this, and with the dot waiting between my front teeth, pressed my open mouth to hers. Her tongue snuck out and took the Dot, licking along my bottom lip. I tangled my tongue with hers and the candy. That was it for me. Charley Cherry was my new favorite flavor.

I snaked my hands into her hair and went all in, teeth clacking, tongues dueling, deep, deep kisses. I explored her mouth to the fullest. My tongue counted every one of her teeth and found her tonsils. The movie and the theater and the popcorn were all gone. It was just me and this fucking hot girl making out in the dark.

Goddess above, she was driving me crazier than any other girl ever had. My wolf certainly hadn't ever perked up and made its wishes known before. I'd like to do a way more with her in the dark. Or better yet, with the lights on so I could stare my fill of her amazing tits and her full ass. God, that ass. I grabbed a hold of her hip and pulled her closer.

"Ow." She laughed. The damn armrest was in the way and in this old-school theater, it wasn't going anywhere. I could rip it right off using just a tenth of my wolf's strength, but just like on the field, I kept that part of me reined in.

A quick glance at the screen told me we'd been making out for a good half of the movie. I'd happily spend the whole movie with my hands down pants and my lips locked to hers. But she'd mentioned she really liked this one, and I didn't want to be the asshole who made her miss it because I was horny as fuck.

Instead of sticking my tongue down her throat some more, I held up the box of candy and offered her another one. She smiled and picked out another red one, tempting me.

I tried to watch the movie, honestly. But this could

have been my first viewing of *The Shining* in the theater, and I still wouldn't be able to pay attention. I didn't care if Jack was a dull boy. I wanted Charley to be mine.

She was rapt with the movie, so instead of trying to kiss her again, I pushed her hair back and started nibbling on her ear. That was the worst and best idea I've ever had. I could practically taste the skin at her throat begging me to bite and mark her.

"Mmm. Wow, that... that feels amazing. Do that again." She moved her head to the side, giving me more access to her delicious skin.

I was dumb, so, so incredibly stupid. I'd been looking forward to this all-night horror fest and an evening off of all the pressures of being the star quarterback, straight-A student, alpha heir to the pack for a month. I could get laid anytime.

Except that's not what it felt like with Charley. I'd just fucking met the girl and I was half in love with her already. She was more than a quick lay. I didn't know why, but she was. She was the kind of girl I'd give up Hitchcock for. She was also the only girl I'd ever been with who wouldn't want me to.

I wanted her. Not just in my bed tonight, either. "Char, I've got *Wolf Man* on my computer."

Charley froze. She stiffened right up and pulled away from me. Yep. I was officially a dumb ass. I should have just been happy to hang out and watch the movie, make out a little and not push her to come home with me. I knew I had a reputation as a ladies' man. She probably thought she was just going to be another notch in my belt.

For the first time ever, that bothered the hell out of me.

Charley glanced over at me, back at the screen for a long time, and then back to me again. "You want me... to go home with you?"

Go big or go home. Alone.

"Yeah. We don't have to do anything you don't want to. We really can just watch the movie, just without these between us." I knocked on the old wooden arm rest.

"Shhh!" Some guy sitting in the middle of the theater turned and glared at us.

Charley stuck her tongue out at him. So fucking cute. She tilted her head to the side a little bit and looked up at me through her lashes, all cute and shy like. "What if I did go home with you?"

Oh, fuck yeah.

"We can do whatever you want." I was about to make a huge fool out of myself. "'Cuz, I like you, Char. I definitely want to take you home and I'd really love to take you to bed, but I also enjoy hanging out with you. I meant what I said. We can just go watch nerdy horror movies at my house. No expectations on my part for anything more."

Those pretty lashes fluttered again. "What if I wanted to do more?"

"Then we'll do more. Like this." I brushed my lips over her throat. My fangs dropped, and I dragged them so gently across the beat of her heart, bee-bopping in her neck, then down across her collarbone. Despite the push of my wolf to mark her and make her mine, not to mention the armrest poking into my intestines I leaned over and slipped my hand along her ribs and underneath her shirt, caressing the small of her back just above where her skin met her panties. "And this."

"Would you two please get a room or shut the hell up?"

We both ducked down, and Charley snickered. "I can't believe I'm going to say this, but my vote is let's get a room."

CHARLIZE

*E*li and I snuck out of the theater so as not to raise the ire of the guy whose movie we'd probably already ruined. Once outside, we practically ran to my car.

"Where too?"

"Over by Greek Row. I share a house with a couple of other guys from the team. But don't worry. They'll either be out or in their rooms at this time of night."

Can't say I relished a walk of shame in the morning past the football team, but we couldn't go back to my place. I also shared a house, but it was only two bedrooms and four girls, so we shared the bedroom. But you know what? Fuck society. I wasn't doing a walk of shame in the morning. I wasn't even sure I was going to sleep with Eli. Even if I did, I wasn't going to be ashamed of it.

He was sweet and nice, and totally unlike what I expected the star quarterback to be like. He'd been a gen a knight in shining Under Armour. I hadn't been looking for that in a guy. In fact, I'd always wanted the opposite.

I'm a strong independent woman, dammit. I don't need a man to rescue me, and most guys take a look at my plus-size curves and don't have any desire to.

Except for Eli.

I also thought we'd tear each other's clothes off the second we got into his room. I was a little bit nervous about that. No t-shirt to hide my muffin top, no jeans to smooth out the cellulite on my thighs. Turned out I didn't have to worry.

Eli showed me to his room, and then stood in the doorway while I looked around. He held his hands at his side like he didn't know what to do with them. I was pretty sure he did. There was that whole wolf in the sheets reputation he had. No way Eli Teagan was nervous to have me in his room.

"Sorry, it's kind of a mess. I didn't expect to have anyone over tonight." He grabbed a pile of books off his nightstand and shoved them into a desk drawer.

Weird. He didn't pick up the dirty socks, or the wadded-up papers next to the desk. He cleaned away his books. But he didn't get them all, and I was dying to know what a guy like him reads. "Here, let me help."

I pretended to straighten the remaining books, but I was definitely checking out the titles. H. P. Lovecraft, Robert Louis Stevenson, Mary Shelley, Shirley Jackson. All the horror classics the movies were made from. Then I spied his Kindle.

"Oh, no. You don't have to." He tried to snag the little e-reader from my hands, but I spun and flopped down onto his bed with it. One flick of the screen and it opened up to what looked like the last page of a book. I read aloud, "If you enjoyed Jakob and Ciara's story, there's a bonus epilogue."

I knew this book. I looked up at Eli, who was turning fifty shades of red. "You're reading a dragon shifter and curvy girl romance?"

Eli snatched the Kindle out of my hand. "It's action adventure with dragons and hot sex scenes. What's not to like?"

"You don't have to defend romances to me. It's my favorite genre. I've read that exact book, and the ten more in the series after it. Have you read her wolf books too?"

Eli's face did some weird contortions, and he mentally processed everything I'd just said. His face settled into a humored smirk, which I very much wanted to kiss right off of him. He sat on the bed next to me. "Uh, duh. Chronologically, the wolf series goes before the dragons."

"Yeah, but she published them while she was still in the middle of writing the dragons. Did you know--"

Eli put a finger to my lips. "Uh, uh, uh. No spoilers."

"Come on. I've got your spoiler, right here." I yanked Eli down onto the bed with me. It was a hundred percent fun being so brazen with him. Mostly because he seemed to like it as much as I did.

He was a big, powerful guy and didn't have to move a muscle if he didn't want to. So, it was extra delicious when he did come down onto the bed with me. We were both fully clothed, but his body over mine, pressing me into the soft blankets, had my girly bit on high alert. Like Defcon five... and a half. "Is this a spoiler alert? I want you to kiss me again."

"Nope, not at all. That spoils nothing, because I want

to kiss you again." Eli brushed his lips across mine, not in a kiss, but a tease. "But I told you, we don't have to do anything except watch a movie together."

He rolled off the bed and grabbed a MacBook from his desk. "*Wolf Man*, the 1941 version, of course, or my personal, albeit controversial comedy horror favorite, *An American Werewolf in London*?"

Was I seriously going to have to talk this guy into getting naked with me? I both liked him more for it and wondered if there was something wrong with him... or me. "What? Of course, it's the campy John Landis flick for the win."

I sat up and propped myself up against his pillows. And we watched a movie. And we didn't have sex. He didn't even feel me up. Sigh.

Maybe he was having second thoughts now that he actually had me home and quite literally in his bed. There was one way to find out. Just as David was transforming into a freaky wolf creature, I stuck my hands down his pants.

Eli hissed as I stroked his erection. Also... that answered that question. He was hard as a rock star, hung like one too. He wanted me. Or he had a thing for Nurse Alex Price.

He grabbed my arm. "Char, if you keep that up, we won't be having half as much fun as we could tonight."

I gave him a little squeeze, and his eyes crossed. "I'm just getting the fun started is all."

In a blink, Eli had the laptop closed and on the floor, his body on top of mine, and my arms up and over my head. He kissed that spot along my collar bone he'd discovered at the theater again and I shivered. He chuckled because he knew I liked it. "Are you sure? We don't--"

The guy was about to give me a complex. I appreciated he was being a good guy and making me not feel pressured, but come on. I couldn't be a whole lot more ready and willing. "If you say we don't have to do anything I don't want to again, I'm going to, to--"

I didn't get to decide what torture I was going to inflict on him because Eli kissed me so deep and long and thoroughly, I forgot all about being worried or mad or anxious. He kept my wrists held in one of his big hands and used the other to slowly push my shirt up.

God. Did he really have to start his exploration of my body with my belly?

Yes. Yes, he did. Eli leaned down and swirled his tongue around my belly button and dipped in. I'd be worried about belly button lint, except he distracted me by kissing, licking, and nibbling his way up my stomach to where my shirt still covered my breasts. "Babe, you can say stop whenever you want, even if you think I don't want to."

"Don't stop." My voice was all sexy and breathy.

He let go of my arms and whipped my shirt right up and over my head. Thank goodness it was laundry day, and I had my one cute bra on because it was the only one left.

"Green polka dots are cute and all, but I've been dying to taste your nipples since our first kiss." He didn't do some kind of bad boy magic and whip my bra off. He pulled the cups down and licked one nipple until I was writhing underneath him.

"Fuck, I could get lost in your tits." He kissed his way across and gave the same treatment to the other breast.

Whatever reputation this guy had, it was well earned. I hadn't even taken my pants off yet and my panties were soaked. "Eli, take your shirt off. I want to touch you too."

"Hmm. It's my turn right now to get you as hot for me as I am for you. Once my clothes come off, I want you wet and ready for me."

Any more ready and I was going to come just from his kisses. "I'm wet. I'm ready."

"Not even close." He finally let go of my wrists and my hands went straight for my pants or his pants, or both at the same time.

Eli pushed my fumbling fingers away and undid the button and pulled down the zipper of my jeans. He grabbed the waistband and started working them down my hips. He hadn't balked at my belly or the stretch marks on my boobs. I guess I wasn't going to freak out that he was about to see my hips and ass in all their plus-size glory.

I lifted my butt, and Eli pulled my jeans down. Before they got to my knees, he gave me a sideways look. "Are you wearing Slytherin panties?"

"Of course, they match the bra, and that's my house. Why, what are you? You're totally a Gryffindor. I can't tell."

"Something like that." He pulled my jeans off and tossed them to the floor, then he ran his fingers along the bottom edge of my undies, getting closer and closer to the center. "Fuck, you're fucking beautiful."

Aww. Not the most romantic turn of phrase, but coming from him with this sort of awe and wonder in his eyes, I'd take it over anything Jane Austen or any other romance writer ever wrote.

He kissed my belly again, lower this time, just above the waistband of my underpants. That sent tingles and butterflies and butterflies with the tingles all through my stomach and down between my legs. Eli grabbed the edge of the fabric between his teeth and pulled them down. I almost giggled until he shredded them with his teeth and licked his way between my legs.

Oh. Oh God. Was he going to...? God bless every chick who had ever been with this man before me and had taught him what women wanted. I wasn't super experienced, but this was college and I'd done my fair share of dorm room hopping and having mediocre sex in the middle of the night. Not once had a guy offered to go down on me.

I wasn't about to admit that either. Not that I could because within a couple of minutes, Eli had me seeing stars. Like actual, literal sparkles flying through my vision as he gave me the best freaking orgasm of my life. His tongue and lips and fingers eeked every last pounding, pulsing, name-screaming ounce of life out of me.

I was still breathing hard when he finally quit and crawled up my body. "You're the absolute most delicious thing I've ever eaten."

Just to prove it. He kissed me and I got the first taste of

my own flavor mixed with the salty taste of him. I would never be able to eat popcorn or Dots again without getting wet.

Having Charley in my bed was better than throwing a game winning pass, better than when Mina goes for Dracula over Harker, better than hot fucking apple pie à la mode from the Sleepy Folk's pie shop in Rogue. I never wanted to leave, and I didn't want her to either.

Her face was flushed, and her eyes were all dreamy. She pushed her hands into my hair and scraped them across my scalp, kissing me back just as deeply. She whispered against my lips, "Do you have condoms?"

Boxes full. God Bless a sexy, confident woman in bed. I wanted her so bad I could hardly see straight and here she was the one taking this to the next level.

I didn't need protection, since wolf-shifters didn't get human diseases and we couldn't pass them on either. Hooray for shifter immunity. Unless this was a full moon and we were mated, she couldn't get pregnant either. But it wasn't like I went around telling all the ladies that and

I'd never want them to feel unsafe in my bed. So, I kept a steady supply in the house. "Yeah. But we don't—"

"Don't try to talk me out of it. I want to feel you inside of me. I want you to feel as good as I do right now. I want you."

My heart exploded. Like right there in my chest. It went kaboom and melted into a puddle of goo. Plenty of girls had said they wanted me. Charley was the first one I believed wanted me for me. The me she knew about, anyway.

Fuck. Should I tell her now who and what I really was?

I was never fucking letting her go. She was mine. I knew it down to my soul. But for the first time in my life, I was worried about being a notch on someone else's belt. It had been ground into me from birth, never to reveal my true self. Wolves mate with other wolves. Not humans.

Only a handful of the highest-ranking wolves had claimed humans as their true mates. How the hell did they go about telling them. That wasn't something I could consider right now. I'd figure it out later. Right now, I was about to send my girl to the moon with more orgasms than she could count.

I rolled off the bed, shucked my clothes, and grabbed the box of condoms out of the desk drawer where I'd shoved the books. I hadn't wanted anyone to know I was reading for pleasure because that wasn't what the cool kids did. Charley didn't care. Actually, she cared and liked the same stuff I did. Stuff I hid from everyone else in my life because it didn't help me get a scholarship, lead a pack, get into the NFL, or get good grades.

For the first time in as long as I could remember, I

wanted to talk to someone about what I liked and wanted to hear what she thought. I was already looking forward to a lot of long nights between her legs and then talking about what was between the pages of the books we were reading.

Look at me. Thinking about a long-term relationship. From one-night stands to night one with my true mate.

I slid a condom on and crawled back into bed. My cock was aching for her, had been all night. But this was more than a fuck. I liked more than her body and that was a way bigger turn on than I ever expected.

I spread Charley's knees and notched the head of my cock at her entrance. "I want this to feel good for you, babe. So, tell me what you like and what you don't. I'm gonna learn your body better than anything else in my four years of college."

She wiggled her hips and pushed the tip of me inside of her hot, waiting pussy. "Is it weird of me to say you're hung like a romance novel hero?"

"I've read romances. That's a damn compliment and an ego boost." I slowly pushed into her and good Goddess, she felt amazing.

She bit her lip, and I struggled to hold myself still so she could adjust. She wasn't wrong about my size. I'd spent enough time in locker rooms to know I had the goods.

"More, Eli." She panted the words. "I want more of you."

"You're so fucking tight. I don't want to hurt you." My wolf was pushing against me, driving me to flip her over, fuck her hard and fast with her ass in the air and her face in the pillows. For the first time in my life, I felt the alpha in me rise up, wanting and needing her submission.

"You aren't, I promise. Please, move. I'm going to go crazy." She wrapped her arms around my shoulders and dug her nails into my back.

Fuck. She was so hot and slick and sliding in and out of her pussy was like heaven. It wouldn't take me long to get close to coming, but there was no way I was going to come until she did. "Slide your hand between us. Feel me pushing into you and rub your clit. I need to feel your pussy squeezing me."

She did exactly what I told her to, and it took only a few flicks of her fingers and a couple of my thrusts and her back was arching up off the bed. "Oh God, Eli. Yes, yes."

The look on her face alone could have gotten me off. I pounded into her, taking us both over the edge. "Charley, fuck, you feel so good. God, yes. Fuck. I fucking love you."

My brain went haywire and the knot at the base of my cock enlarged. I shoved myself into her so deep I could feel her entire cunt coming around me. Never had I felt anything like this. My orgasm hit like a fucking thunderbolt, smashing into a freight train, crashing into a mountain. My vision tunneled and my heart pounded against my chest. Or was that my wolf?

The beast inside was pushing me to mark her, claim her, and make her mine.

I dropped my head to her shoulder and used my last bit of strength to keep myself from sinking my fangs into her, marking as mine. It took all I had not to collapse on top of her.

I could hardly breathe. I couldn't move.

No, like I legitimately couldn't move. The wolf's knot had gone full-on beast mode mating, and we were stuck together until my animal nature was satisfied she was mine.

I just told a girl I'd met a few hours ago that I loved her.

And I fucking meant it.

That was crazy, and I was a serious asshole. What the hell was she going to think of me now? Shit. She hadn't said anything back. It's not like I expected her to say she loved me back. I slowly raised my head to see what her reaction was, praying it wasn't revulsion. That she hadn't freaked the fuck out when she realized my cock was no ordinary human one and I'd just busted right out of the god-damned condom.

"Char? I...." Her eyes were closed, her breathing soft and even. She was asleep. "Charley?"

Well, hell. I'd fucked her into a coma. There was a dickhead part of me that was patting myself on the back for that. There was another part that was hoping and praying she hadn't heard me. I wasn't waking her up to find out, either.

I carefully held myself over her, so as not to squish her with my bulk, and had a long talk with my wolf. Which was weird since the wolf was me. I was the wolf. There was no real separation between the two parts of myself and I'd never felt more like I had a split personality than just now.

Look, wolf. She's not ready. If I reveal myself to her now, she's going to think I'm a monster and freak the fuck out. I don't want to scare her or hurt her. She knows nothing about the supernatural. If I'm going to talk her into being my mate, I need to ease her into this world.

The knot pulsed, pleasure rolling through me like a freaking orgasm aftershock. Oh, yeah. The wolf wasn't ready to let her go without a fight.

Char sighed so adorably that I quit fighting and pulled a blanket over us. I had no fucking idea what was going to happen in the morning, in the light of day. I'd never cared before. Girls came and went from my bed, from my life.

I wanted this one to stay. But she didn't know what I was.

My wolf didn't care.

How in the hell was I going to tell her? The beast pushed against me, and my skin and bones tingled with the magic of the shift.

No. Nuh-uh. Absolutely not. I was not having her wake up with a monster breathing and slobbering in her face. It took long, deep breaths to halt the shift, and I got another near orgasm pulsing in my cock for it. The knot swelled even larger, and Charlie's eyelashes fluttered.

Fuck.

Even without taking my animal being right in her face, she'd still realize there was something going on with me. My fangs were out, my eyes glowed with the magic inside of me, and with as much pleasure as was throbbing through my cock, I was on the verge of fucking her again.

Because I'm an asshole. Shit. I will not be that guy. Now the problem is not just how to tell Charlie, it's how to appease my beast to give me the time to figure everything out. Not only is everyone else in my life pressuring me, my wolf is, too.

I can escape my family, I can hide from the team for a night, but I can never escape the wolf. It won't back down until I do something to make Charlie mine.

Goddess, help me.

I pressed my lips to her throat, exactly where I would mark her. No matter how much my wolf pushed me, I would not mark her without her consent. She knew nothing about my world or what marking, claiming, or mating meant.

I couldn't help it and scraped my fangs across her skin. She shivered, and I wrapped her arms around my neck, pulling me closer.

"Ooh, again? You're an animal." She pushed her hips against mine and groaned.

This, I could do. I rocked my hips, knowing I couldn't pull out, but I had other skills. Within a minute, I had her eyes rolling back in her head and her cunt fluttering around my cock once again. Before I knew it, my balls tightened, and I came hard right along with her.

Then she did something I totally didn't expect. She growled and bit my neck.

She bit me. She fucking marked… me. I could feel the

magic tingling from her to me, across my skin and deep into my soul.

Like nothing else could, that satisfied my beast.

I wasn't sure how to feel about it. She wasn't a shifter. I would have been able to scent that on her. Charlie was a full-blooded American human woman. What the fuck was going on?

When she released me from her bite, she kissed my neck and then ran her thumb over it. "Oops. I gave you a hickey. Couldn't help myself."

"Next time, I'll give you one." She had no idea how much I meant that. I pulled out of her body and rolled over, wrapping her in my arms, tucking her head onto my shoulder. She was asleep in a few minutes again and I was in wonder of her ability to pass the fuck out.

I laid there, holding her tight in my arms, overthinking everything, letting all the pressures of the world pile on, and on, and on until the sun hit me smack in the face. Morning already. Ugh.

Charley was still and softly snoring. She had the cutest sexy bed hair, and I'd bet money my pillows were going to smell like her. I might never do laundry again.

I was gonna pull a pussy ass move and sneak out of here before she woke up. Put the ball in her court. I'd leave her a note and if she wanted to see me again, she could. If not.

I always had football and the whole damn world's high expectations to fulfill.

I dressed quietly and put her clothes on the desk chair. All except her adorable Slytherin undies. Those went into my pocket. With a quick scrawl on a sheet of notebook paper, I had my note.

> *Char,*
>
> *You were sweeter than anything last night.*
>
> *If I didn't have to get to practice, I'd happily spend all day in bed with you watching every version of Stephen King's It.*
>
> *As always, no pressure. But if you want to see where this is going, swing by the field house any time today and we can talk.*
>
> *Or do more.*
>
> *--E*

I wanted to make sure she saw it. Aha. I pulled one of the precious sleeves of mini donuts from my secret stash, that no respecting quarterback would have, and propped the note up against them. Then I made my way out of there as fast and as quiet as I could.

I caught a break because the other guys were already gone, off to the gym by this time. Coach liked us to do a light workout the days after a game, and the earlier we got it done, the earlier we were free. Except for me and few other key players. We got to watch film reels and pick over every god-damned mistake we made.

I hit the gym first and got the side-eye from my roommates. Shit. They surrounded me like a pack challenging an alpha.

They'd definitely seen Charley's car still parked in front of the house this morning. We'd all agreed at the beginning of the school year that no girls stayed overnight. I'd pissed plenty of cheerleaders off by taking them home in the middle of the night.

I put in my earbuds and started the twenty-minute warm up routine on the treadmill, to hold them off. That didn't work even a smidgen.

Ty, my well-meaning teammate number one, said, "Tell us she was too drunk to drive, so you took her home and she's coming back to get her car later."

I shook my head and upped the speed to give them the hint I wasn't in the mood to talk. "We weren't drinking."

"So, she's back at the house?" Luka, well-meaning roommate number two, asked.

"Probably." Fuck, this was uncomfortable. I was not used to being the one who broke the rules. We didn't bring non-shifter girls home. I knew that. We all knew better. We didn't even room with non-shifter teammates.

"Human chicks are a distraction you can't afford, man." Luka shook his head at me like I was a disappointment. "Fuck 'em and blow off some steam, sure. But don't be thinking you're finding a mate or some shit."

"I know, I know." They were right. My parents were counting on me playing a little pro sports before I came home to take over the pack with some money in my pockets. It was all about prestige and positioning, with so many powerful packs on the East Coast.

But none of these assholes understood what happened between me and Charley last night. I didn't fucking care if this blew my career.

My whole life was about everyone else's expectations for me. I wanted one god-damned thing for myself. I'd gotten a taste of life without all the pressure of my peers and teachers and coaches and family. Gotten a taste of Charley.

"You're going to taint your pack's pure lineage for the fat, nerdy girl? Dude, you didn't already tell her you 're a wolf shifter, did you?"

And just then she walked into the gym. Shit, if she'd been a shifter herself, she probably would have heard everything we said. I glared at the bunch of them with my best shut-the-fuck-up face.

Kirill slugged me in the arm hard and pointed at Charley. "She must give some pretty damn good head, because there is no way you could fit your big old dick between those thunder thighs."

The other guys made the appropriate oohs and ahhs that went with the burn. All I could feel was the heat of a thousand suns on my face. Char had heard every fucking word, and the look on her face was breaking my heart.

She was hurt and scared. Of me and my asshole teammates.

I balled up my fists and literally shook with the rage. One more word from any of these assholes and I was going to shift right here in the campus gym and rip all their throats out.

Charley turned on her heel and ran out of the gym. I'd go after her as soon as I got myself under control. The best way to do that was to let out this pent-up rage on Kirill's face.

I knew better than to break my hand on his face. I used enough of my wolf's agility to jump over the tread-mill's handrail and spun on the balls of my feet, switching direction faster than he could even blink to crack him across the jaw with my elbow.

He dropped to the floor like Tyson in the tenth at the Tokyo Dome. The rest of the group backed away as they should. I didn't even wait around, just took off after Charley. Either that girl was secretly a track star, or she had a penchant for hiding. The quad was wide open, and she was nowhere to be seen.

I jogged toward the student center, trying to find that sweet scent of hers in the air. I could track her if I caught even a hint of her scent. Maybe she went to hide in the library. I'd lose her in there since she already smelled of books. Shit.

Maybe she went back to my house? That was the opposite direction, but I could still catch her. We only lived a ten-minute walk from campus. I could get there in two if I sprinted the whole way, which I did. Her car was gone.

Fuck.

Fucking fuckety fuckballs. I didn't even have her phone number, email, snapchat. Nothing. I didn't even know her last name.

I should have known better. I did know better. But my hormones got the best of me. That had to be it. Because I was smart and didn't date or sleep with asshole jocks. Or dumbasses who thought they were actual dire wolves.

I'm so sure. *"You didn't already tell her you're a wolf shifter, did you?"*

Give me a break.

I never should have let anyone in the whole wide world know about my love of horror movies. Especially not some cocky jock. I saw him freeze up, and that gave me get the chance to get the hell out of the gym and the awkward morning after.

But what if... no. But... maybe? Did I believe in supernatural beings? A little bit. I was honest enough with myself that some of my love of the horror genre was that layer of what if. He had growled at me during sex.

Oh. My. God. What was wrong with me? Werewolves were not real.

Probably.

I hid behind the door like the big fat coward I was. I didn't want to hear any excuses about why he thought it was okay for his friends to make fun of my hobbies and especially not diss me and my body. Asshats.

Eli took off running toward the quad, sniffing the air like a drug dog. I waited until he was out of sight and beat feet to my car.

What I needed now was to escape into a good romance novel and forget about my non-existent love life. Except, crap. I'd left my book at Eli's house. I thought he might like the sports romance I'd just picked up. Dumb.

Fine. I steered my car instead to the coffee shop. The second I walked into The Moon Bean, I breathed a sigh of relief. Nothing like the smell of coffee and books to heal a broken heart. I was definitely not taking home a paranormal romance tonight.

"Uh-oh. I know that look. The date didn't go well?" Selena, the owner, came around the corner with a pile of books as high as her head. She'd said she wanted to expand the bookshop side of the business, but geez.

I grabbed a stack off the top, so they didn't all go tumbling to the ground. I'd a hundred percent forgotten about the date from hell. That felt like a thousand years ago and not last night. "Yeah. No. That guy was the worst."

"Hmm... yeah. I knew he wasn't the right one. But at least you got out there and now I don't have to fire you." She set her books down on the counter and started sorting them by author to put to the three new shelves we'd just gotten in.

A. How did she know that guy wasn't the right one

and why didn't she tell me? And B. I'd thought for a hot minute that Eli was my guy. Should I tell Selena about him? No, definitely not. "You weren't really going to fire me, were you?"

"Hmm. It would be tempting." She tapped her finger on her temple. "I hate to see a girl like you be miserable, so I would have to let you go just so I didn't have to look at you moping around our brand new romance section every day."

A girl like me? What was that supposed to mean? But to be fair, I had made plans to mope around today. A new section of the store dedicated to shatter-my-heart-and-make-me-cry romance novels sounded like just the right place to do that. Sigh.

"That guy didn't break your heart or something, did he? I should have told you, but it wasn't the time. I will march right over to that bar and—" Selena brandished a book with a hot shirtless Viking holding a sword on the cover.

"No, no. It's not him that broke my heart." What was I thinking? That Eli was actually like a book boyfriend, all perfect and loving?

I fucking love you.

He'd said those words to me. I'd been too much of a chicken to say them back. Good thing. He clearly didn't mean it. Heat of the moment, I guess. Whatever. I didn't need Eli Teagan in my life.

Selena narrowed her eyes at me and sniffed. "Spill it."

I came straight here and without a shower. Did I smell like hot, schmexy sex? Crap. I backed away. "No. Everything is fine. I am perfectly happy getting a degree in literature with an emphasis on nineteenth century British authors, working at the coffee shop, stocking books, and avoiding boys for the rest of my life. I chose the wrong guy to give my heart to, so..."

I'd get a plant, and maybe a parrot. I'd teach the bird to say funny things like "I vant to suck your blood." and "RedRum, RedRum."

I could have long conversations with the ficus that would be just as intelligent as with any football player. Except Eli was smarter and funnier than a ficus. He'd get the horror movie reference I taught my parrot to say. If he even liked horror movies, that is.

Selena smacked the book down on the counter with a smack. "You're fired."

"What?" My face and hands went all cold and numb, then heated right back up as I got mad. "Because some guy who was clearly too hot for me treated me like dog poo?"

"No. Because I thought you were smarter than that. You're loud and proud and confident and never let anyone treat you like... poo, did you say?"

What? Like... is that what Selena, this badass take-no-shit woman, who pushed the rest of us to go after what we wanted, thought I was confident?

"You know who you are and what you like, and you've let no one else tell you otherwise. Not even fate." The tingle of the door opening and a new customer walking in sounded, but we both ignored it. Selena shook her head and rolled her eyes at me. "Why is it different with boys? What in the world makes you think you'd ever choose to open up to the wrong guy?"

Whatever. A love of horror movies and being good in bed does not a wonderful boyfriend make. He wasn't even my boyfriend, for goodness sake. He was a stupid one-night stand, and I was locker talk. That's not fate.

"I'm not the wrong guy. I swear to you Charley."

I spun toward the door and there was Eli, shirtless like he'd been at the gym, sweaty, and with an unnatural glow in his eyes. Were those fangs popping out from under his top lip?

Selena clapped her hands. "Ooh, I knew it. I just knew it."

I frowned at her. "Knew what?"

"And it's not even the full moon yet. Damn, I'm good. This is so going on WolfSpace later." Selena legit just walked away from me and Eli, talking to herself and ignoring me and my questions all together.

"Charley, I'm not sure what all you heard back there —" Eli stepped closer and reached out.

Nope. I turned sideways. "I heard everything, and I do not enjoy being made fun of."

"Shit. Everything?"

I folded my arms and gave him the stink-eye channeling my inner loud, proud, and confident woman Selena said I had inside. "Everything."

He swallowed hard. "Okay. Uh... let me explain."

"Explain how big of dicks your so-called friends are?" I was down for having him do some groveling.

"Yeah," he groused and cupped his neck, right where I'd given him a hickey. "That and... the uh, other thing."

"Like I believe that you're a wol—" Wait a second. "What's wrong with your neck, Eli?"

I pushed his hand to the side and where there should be a reddish bruise from my over-exuberance last night, there was a swirl of black and gray, like ink. I ran my fingers gently over his skin, in awe of what I was seeing. The marks were forming shapes, as if a magic spell worked on his skin. A wolf inside of a crescent moon appeared.

A wolf with glowing purple eyes.

"Eli?"

"Touch me like that again, Charley." His voice had gone down a full octave, and he was breathing a hell of a lot faster than a second ago.

Eli's irises were glowing with that exact same purple light, but his pupils were so huge I could see my reflection. I brushed my fingers over what now looked like a live moving tattoo. "I'm still mad at you, but what's going on? Is this some kind of prank you all pull on poor, unsuspecting one-night stands to get rid of us?"

Eli grabbed my hand and kissed the inside of my wrist. "You're not a one-night stand. At least, I don't want you to be. What the guys said about being wolf shifters, they weren't kidding."

"You're not getting out of this by distracting me with your horror cosplay fantasies or by turning me on with your well-placed kisses. Do we need to call an ambulance? Maybe an exorcist?"

"No, babe. Listen. I'm being serious, and —"

The bell above the door jingled again, and I pushed Eli toward the bookshelves. If he was having some kind of weird health problem and-or mental health attack, that was no one else's business.

"Hey, you, Eli Teagan. I've got a bone to pick with you, man." The douchepotato from last night stumbled into the coffee shop. He was three sheets to the wind, and it was barely afternoon. He was a real winner, winner, chicken dinner. That's what I get for going out on a date with the first guy who even vaguely flirts with me. I sure know how to pick 'em.

Eli stepped around me and pushed me behind him. "You don't want to do this, man."

The way he emphasized the word man was weird. Did these two know each other or was this just a dick measuring contest? Either way, I did not like being in the middle of it. "I think you could use a cup of coffee, my guy. It's on the house."

Bad date dude, whose name I couldn't remember for the life of me, snapped and snarled at me. "Stay out of this, you traitorous whore."

Uh, why were his eyes glowing like a wild animal caught in the headlights? Something was seriously wackadoo here. I needed to find Selena and call the police. Or maybe animal control. Or even Sam and Dean Winchester.

I glanced up at Eli to see if he'd caught that too or if I was hallucinating. And that didn't make me feel any better because his eyes were glowing too, but with an almost neon purple. When the hell had his freshly shaved face gone beyond five o'clock shadow? Holy shit, those were a canine style fang poking out from his upper lip.

Eli was a real life wolf man.

Cue the dreadful horror movie music where the heroine makes a dumb mistake and dies.

"Watch it, asshole." I stalked toward the guy who Charley had been harassed by last night. Fuck, was it seriously only last night? My gut told me I'd known her for a lifetime.

A lifetime together is what we'd get if I had my way. Just as soon as I took care of this douchecanoe and begged for Charley's forgiveness, on my hands and knees, if I had to.

The bad date dude was about to hulk out and in front of a human who knew nothing of the supernatural aspects of the world. That was not only dumb, it was arrogant. Which meant he was a god-damned one-blood. Assholes who thought shifters were superior and that humans should be subservient to us.

My father had dealt with them during the worst of the pack wars. He'd warned me they were dangerous. Dangerous because they were stupid and didn't think for themselves. Blindly followed the dogma of the worst of the Volkovs.

This was my school, and I didn't want anyone of his ilk tainting our safe haven for higher education. Charley was my girl. Pieces of shit like him didn't belong anywhere near someone as special as her. It made me sick to think he'd ever touched her.

I kept my voice low, hoping Charley wouldn't hear, or if she did wouldn't understand. I'd explain about shifters and our society as soon as I could, but surprising her with it wasn't just dumb, it was against the code we wolves all followed. Punishable by death. "If you're challenging me for my mate, this is not the time nor the place."

"Why the fuck would you want to claim a human for a mate? Is the whole Chincoteague pack pussy whipped by these weakling human women?" Bad date dude sucked on his front teeth and shot a glance at Charley. "Or do you just want to fuck her? I'm happy to share her with you."

Okay, you want to play that game, fucker. I growled so deep and low that the alpha in me was ready to bust out and tear this beta to shreds for stepping out of line. Penalties be damned. "She is mine."

"Excuse me? I belong to no man... or beast." Charley snapped at us both. That's my girl. At least she didn't come out and get between us. Instead, she called for backup. Because she was a smart cookie, and I was being dumber than a box of rocks. "Selena, I think you need to come out here."

"I'm right here, *umnyashka*. I had to go close the shades and lock the door. Can't have any ball bunnies or campus security interfering with a challenge." Selena, who had definitely not been there a minute ago, popped out from behind one bookshelf and thankfully hauled Charley back a few feet. "We're in for a show. It's very exciting having two young strapping wolves fight over you. Ah, how I miss the good old days. Oh, stand back, I think that beta is in for an ass-whooping by your handsome alpha heir."

Yeah, he was. If Selena Troika, matriarch of the most powerful pack in the world and mother to the Wolf Tzar, was down for a challenge happening right here, right now, on her turf, I was going full fangs ahead. Beta one-blood boy needed to learn a lesson on how to treat women, human or wolf. Except that meant shifting, and Charley wasn't ready for that yet. Shit. Okay, so no shifting then.

"What? You mean wolves like raw, raw, go get 'em Bay State Dire Wolves, right?" Uh-oh. Char sounded a little hysterical and I couldn't do a damn thing to comfort her right now.

No, I had to make sure she was safe and protected from the likes of this guy. I narrowed my eyes at my opponent and snarled. Fucker needed to back off. He knew better. Or maybe not, because he hunched down and started circling like he was looking for a spot to attack.

"This is the best part. Now watch and keep an open mind." I couldn't take the chance to even take my eyes off this beta, but I could smell the popcorn and distinct giddiness. Like we were about to put on a show.

The scent of excitement wasn't coming from Charley, though. "Open mind? About boys fighting over me?"

"Just remember, the Goddess wouldn't have chosen you as a fated mate if she didn't think you couldn't handle it," Selena said like it was no big deal. Oh, that's right. To her, it wasn't. She was the head of the family that started the revolution. Before her sons, no one mated humans.

She broke all the rules, and I'd never broken a single one.

Maybe that needed to change.

Beta boy lunged for me, and I easily spun around him. He faltered on his feet, and I wondered what in the hell kind of training his pack gave him before sending him off to college. Not anything that involved agility. Probably didn't even hunt for himself.

His back was to the ladies now and from this position I could monitor them and d-bag at the same time. I gave Charley a wink and Selena a nod of thanks-for-the-solidarity.

"If you're gonna pick a weakling girl over your own kind, oh mighty golden boy, then you've made the wrong fucking choice." Beta boy's wolf shone in his eyes and was too close to the surface.

I should thank Selena, because I didn't care if the Volkovs themselves came and tried to tell me what to do. For the first time in my whole damn life, I was making a choice for myself. Not for my family, not for my pack, but for me. And my choice was Charley.

Assuming I didn't scare the shit out of her in the next ten seconds. I let my wolf push up and out. I'd chosen Charley as my mate, but ultimately it was up to her, and she couldn't make an informed decision if she didn't know who and what I was.

Beta boy may be forcing me into this, but that was a good thing. No time like protecting one's mate to expose the secrets entrusted to us all.

"What in the world is going on here? Have you all lost or minds or is this some kind of fraternity prank?" Charley's voice was nearing nuclear meltdown. I stared directly into her eyes and pushed my thoughts of love and lust toward her, hoping she'd get the message and not freak out.

My stomach went all tingly, and then my skin followed suit. Right in front of the first woman I cared anything about, I stripped naked, prepared to show her my true form, let her see the real me. The wolf, the alpha, her one true mate.

Selena took a bite of popcorn, and Charley's eyes went wide. "What in the actual hell? Is this actually a dick-measuring contest? I'd only been joking about that before."

Beta boy did the same and we both let the wolves take over. I dropped to all fours and let the bones break and reform, my fur burst through my skin, and my wolf senses take over. All without taking my eyes off Charley.

Her mouth dropped open, but Selena shoved a few kernels of popcorn in, forcing Char to chew. "Open mind, dear, not open mouth."

I wanted to trot over and push my nose into her hand, let her touch me, and maybe even stroke behind my ears. I would have if Beta boy hadn't decided to try his luck against me. He lunged and Char yelped. That almost distracted me, but both my wolf and the athlete in me knew how to turn off distractions in the heat of battle. If ever I needed my head in the game, this was it.

Before Beta boy got anywhere near my mate, I leaped into the air and tackled him to the ground, grabbing his throat in my teeth. Charley gasped, and I prayed to the Goddess of the Moon that I hadn't blown it with her. Please, oh please, oh please, let her be a tough cookie. I was pretty sure she was, but we hadn't known each other long enough to put any pressure on our fresh, shiny, lust-induced relationship.

I had to trust that I'd made the right choice just now, letting her see my wolf. The wolf was cocksure and confident, so I would be, too.

Beta boy struggled, and I gave him another shake. Since he wasn't in my pack and I wasn't yet a full alpha, we couldn't communicate in wolf form, but I growled in a way he should know meant I wanted him to show me his throat and submit to my dominance.

"Get him, Eli." Charley shouted and my heart sang. "Show him we don't take any shit from assholes like him."

That did not sound like a woman afraid of me. I fell all the rest of the way in love with her at that very moment. No one and no wolf would stand between me and my chance at a true mate.

I should have known better than to get that cocky.

Instead of submitting, Beta boy twisted and rolled, swiping his claws across my face. Blood spurted into my eyes, and I couldn't see. It was the advantage this dickbag needed. He slammed into my side, slamming me against the bookshelves and knocking the air out of me.

My wolf would heal my injuries, but nothing could heal my heart when I heard Beta boy's growl and Charley's scream.

It took me all of about three minutes after seeing Eli turn into the most amazing and gorgeous wolf for my brain to stop whirling around like a tornado straight out of Oz. Good thing I had to Good Witch of the South, or, err, of the coffee shop to help me.

Selena was not only not freaking out about two college boys turning in to wolves in the middle of our coffee shop, she'd made popcorn and was cheering Eli on. That is until Bad Date Dude started to win.

I got so mad that such an asshole might hurt the man I loved, even if he was a wolf, I screamed at him.

"Screaming won't help Eli, dear." Selena smirked at me, or maybe she smiled? "What else you got?"

"What else do you expect from me. I don't have fangs and claws." What was I supposed to do? Throw a book at them?

"You've got more power than you give yourself credit for. All women do, we just don't flaunt it like the men. Because we don't have to. Well, until we need to. Then look out." She waggled an eyebrow at me like I was in on some kind of secret with her.

I wasn't. Unless you counted the fact that werewolves existed. "What's my power?"

"What do you think it is?"

"This isn't a therapy session. That dickbag of a bad dog is going to hurt Eli. I need to save him." I didn't give Selena a chance to say anything else cryptic because said dickbag dog was creeping closer to all three of us.

Okay, what was I good at that could be my secret superpower? I was great at reading. Which wasn't useful here, but had exposed me to lots of fresh ideas and worlds. Maybe that's why I wasn't freaked the fuck out that Eli was a wolf. I was gonna go with that theory.

I was good at watching horror movies. Uh, yeah. That was sort of happening right in front of my eyes. Right. I'd seen about a million heroines who were too dumb to live run away from the monsters only to end up getting chased down and eaten. And not in the fun way.

I refuse to be the TDTL girl. What did the girls who lived do?

Aha. They embraced the weird and made friends... or became lovers of the monsters.

Check and mate.

Although, I was not making friends with Bad Date Dude.

I was missing one more piece of the puzzle. Selena cleared her throat and jerked her head at the rapidly approaching bad guy wolf. "Ahem... maybe try some of that loud and proud confidence?"

If Selena believed I had it in me, maybe it was true. I

was fantastic good at being loud and using my words. I should have done so when Eli's dumbass friends were being dumb asses. Eli could have used his words and told me who and what he really was. I never liked the part in the movies where the monster was silenced.

In my best unfreaked out, embracing the weird, and loud and proud way I could muster, I turned on the were-wolf stalking toward me and smacked his nose. "Bad dog. Bad, naughty dog. Don't be a dick."

Bad Date Dude whined and stuck his tail between his legs. Huh. Okay, good. Guess he just needed a good telling off. I had plenty more where that came from.

The bell above the door of the coffee shop rang and in walked Eli's teammates from the gym. Uh-oh. I whispered out the side of my mouth, "I thought you locked the doors."

She whispered back, "I did. But I also called for backup. Your mate is an alpha, and he needed his pack. We're better with our friends and family around us. Why do you think I wanted you to find yours?"

Her eyes glowed a sparkling blue for just a minute, and then she tossed another piece of popcorn into the air and caught it between her teeth. Her very fanglike teeth.

A. Was everyone around here a wolf except for me? Were all these guys wolf shifters too? B. Ahh, Selena set me up. Crafty fox, I mean wolf.

Bad Date Wolf turned into a gray streak and bolted out the door, dashing between the legs of the football team. I had a feeling they could have stopped him if they wanted to. But all eyes were on me and Eli.

Shit. Eli.

I dropped to the floor and set his head in my lap, stroking his ears.

"Lucky bastard. I wish I had a girl who'd do that to do me."

With some creaking and cracking, Eli shifted back into his human form. He had three long scratches from his forehead to his cheek, but they were healing even as I looked at them. "Are you okay?"

I got up, and Eli followed me. Selena threw him his pants, and I'd need to remember to ask him about why he'd stripped down before shifting. "No more shifting today, kids. I've got a business to run."

The lot of them echoed some version of "yes, ma'am," and shuffled their feet until she shooed them toward the coffee counter. Selena re-opened the doors, and it didn't take long before more students filed in. There was an entire line outside.

"Yeah. Thanks to you, sweetness." He put his hand over mine and held it to his cheek. "Are you okay? You're not freaking out?"

"I did for a minute. But I think having a supernatural boyfriend and not freaking out is my superpower. Either that or it's not minding that you were naked in the middle of the coffee shop." I shrugged, and Eli laughed.

"I wanted to tell you, but it's complicated." He sat up and gave me a long, lingering kiss. Until the guys started hooting and hollering.

The asshole who had called me fat was standing right in front of the rest of his buddies. He deserved a good telling off. I'd smack his nose too, but it looked like he'd already hurt himself. Good. "Look here, dickface. I don't know what issues you have in your life that you feel you need to lash out at other people for not fitting into your little preconceived ideals, but I hope you get help with that."

The other guys around laughed and pointed at us like kindergarteners. Lord, save me from dumb jocks. Not that they were all dumb, but these didn't seem to have an original brain cell between them.

"The rest of you might take a good long look at yourselves in the mirror, too. You don't have to be empty-headed robots with no emotions who blindly follow the leader because he's got a big dick." Yes, I meant Eli. If more of them acted like him, I'd probably like them all better.

There were more snickers, but a lot fewer than before. Maybe I was getting through to them. Except they weren't looking at me. Oh... Eli's eyes glowed, his fangs had dropped, and he was snarling at the bunch of them.

I smacked him on the arm. "You could have said something, you know. You could have defended me."

"Doesn't look like you need me to. You put these douchebags in their places just fine. It's one of the things I love about you. You're not like the dumb bunny Barbies I used to go out with."

"Hey," a girl standing in line for coffee shouted. "I'm graduating with honors in theoretical physics and start at NASA in the spring, you bag of dicks."

Eli didn't even glance at the girl who did indeed look like engineer Barbie. He only had eyes for me. He was sexy and staring at my mouth, and did I mention I was suddenly very hot?

"I like that you know who you are and don't put on a facade for the world. Not like I do. Every move I make from the classes I choose to the friends I have is to make sure everyone thinks I'm the golden boy. But I'm not and I'm tired of fucking trying to be." His words were for me, but everyone here could hear him.

He thought I liked who I was. Selena had said the same. I mean, I tried, but I had a mask I showed to the world too. I wasn't hiding a supernatural secret like he was, but there were parts of me I didn't show to the world either. Everyone had that part of themselves they kept secret and safe.

I guess that's why I had fallen for Eli in the first place. We'd both let those walls down and shown each other our real selves, even before I knew he was more than your average bear... boy... whatever. "Eli, don't put me on some pedestal. I've got my own issues. We all do."

I dropped my voice to a whisper. "I understand the parts you have to keep secret, but I don't get why you think you have to hide your actual personality from everyone. You're a cool guy, and I don't just mean because you're the captain of the football team. You're smart and funny and I thought you were a nice guy until you got around these schmoes."

He glanced over at said schmoes and back at me. "Then help me be that guy, Charley."

Sweet. But no can do. "Don't put that on me. You gotta come clean on who you are and what you like all on your own."

Eli sighed and looked over at the other players again.

Their opinions really mattered. I hoped not as much as mine. "Fine."

He stretched his neck from side to side and swung his arms like he was warming up for a game. Then held his arms up to the air like he was declaring his faith. "I like classic horror movies."

"Dude. Who doesn't?" someone shouted from the peanut gallery.

Eli did that face people make when they are both shocked, pleased, and thinking - what the hell?

"Keep going," I prompted him and took a step closer.

His wolf flashed in his eyes again, but he nodded, acknowledging what I was really asking. "I also like nerdy girls with curves that blow my mind."

"Once again, dude. Who doesn't, besides this douchecanoe?" One guy shoved the fat phobic douchecanoe.

I stepped even closer.

Eli blinked a few times, and he licked his lips. I saw the tips of his fangs. He couldn't hide them from me anymore. I didn't want him to.

He hadn't expected his friends to be okay with what he was saying, and it was so cute to see how genuine acceptance hit him in the feels.

"And?"

He lowered his arms and held out a hand to me. "I like this nerdy girl right here, and I'd really like to ask her to be my girlfriend."

"Dude."

Eli turned and pointed at the guys. "Don't even say it."

I took that last step between us and put my arms

around him. "I like this big mysterious guy right here, and I'd really like to be his girlfriend."

Even standing all the way up on my tippy toes, I still had to pull Eli's head down to give him the kiss we both needed.

"Get a room, you two."

Eli smiled against my lips. "I hear there's a werewolf marathon on tonight. Wanna come over?"

"Ahroooo."

"I'll take that as a yes."

ELI

*W*asn't I just the luckiest fucker that ever lived?

This was Thanksgiving weekend, and I had to be back on Saturday to play in the Dire Wolves' game this weekend. That meant only one full day at home with the fam. That wasn't nearly enough time to eat a turkey and introduce my girlfriend, my mate, to my pack.

We were doing it anyway. The drive down to Chincoteague wasn't that long, and I didn't want to wait any longer. Tonight was a full moon, and it had just about killed me not to claim Charley on the last two moons. But I wanted to do this right, in front of my pack, so everyone knew she belonged to me and me to her.

"No, no, no." She wagged her finger at me. But I put her hand back on the wheel before she could get too riled up. "Nobody said anything about having sex in public. Eli Teagan, that is not my kink."

Char had taken to supernatural life like she'd been born to it, even though she wasn't one herself. She was going to make a fantastic matriarch someday. But I had waited to tell her exactly what the mating ritual involved until we were well on our way to my pack's home turf. I guessed on the road, a half hour away, was as close as it got. "Sweetness, it will be fine, I promise. It's not like anyone will watch us. Everyone else there will be getting it on with their mates."

She raised her eyebrow at me in the way that I learned meant I was in trouble. I loved getting her riled up. She was so damn deliciously adorable when she was mad. "So this is an orgy?"

"No. It's a sacred ceremony that has been a tradition for wolf shifters for centuries." Although, I'd kind of always thought of it as the wolf orgy. Not that I'd ever taken part, just watched once I came of age. It felt different this time since she and I would be the ones mating.

I thought I'd be nervous like human grooms always were on TV and movies. Those guys were dumb. I could hardly wait.

The GPS dinged for the turn down the long secluded one-lane road that led to my house, the pack house for the Chincoteague wolves. Char took the right and grinned at me. "You're making that up. You just want to have kinky sex. You could just say that. I've read plenty of erotic romance novels, you know."

Oh, I knew. There was an entire stack of them on my bedside table. Pornhub had nothing on erotic romance authors. "If you want, I can tie you up and blindfold you. The other wolves in my pack might think you're weird, but you're my kind of weird."

"Eli." She groaned and rolled her eyes at me.

She also squirmed in her seat. I easily scented her arousal, and I'd use it to my full advantage if I had to. "I'll lay you down in a soft bed of leaves and tie your hands up over your head so your pretty tits are pushed forward. Your pink little nipples will be hard in the cool night air and just waiting for me to suck on them."

"This isn't working," she sing-songed.

Oh, yes, it was.

"And just when you're ready to beg me to fuck you, I'm going to spread your legs wide and eat that delicious pussy of yours until you're just on the verge of coming in my mouth."

"Uh huh." Her voice was nothing but a whisper now, and I knew I had her. She was rapt, and I was harder than rocks. We might have to make a pit stop before we got to the house.

"But I won't let you. Not until you say that you're mine for everyone to hear." She'd said it a hundred times before. My wolf demanded it from her and she gave it what it wanted because then I could give her lots of orgasms. But tonight was special, because my entire pack would know that I'd found my fated mate.

The first of the Chincoteagues to bring home a human mate.

She stuck out her tongue at me. "Meanie."

"You love it."

Charley blushed, mostly because we both knew it drove her crazy with desire when I kept her on the edge of an orgasm. The waiting made it even more explosive when I made her come after a lot of teasing, wanting, and needing.

There was one part of what would happen tonight at the mating ritual I'd left out. Tonight, I would mark her just as she'd marked me. A bite to the soft spot between her throat and shoulder that called to me like a siren's song. I'd been so close to marking her every time we were together, but I held myself back. Just like Charley, I knew it would be even better for the anticipation. The mark would make her night more than just another fuck...in front of my pack.

We pulled into my parents' driveway a few minutes later and I gave her a quick, hard kiss. "Come on, my mom's dying to meet you."

"What if your dad doesn't approve of me?" My dad had been wary of me bringing home a human, but one call from Selena Troika and he'd changed his tune.

"They're going to love you. Just like I do. You'll see." I dragged her out of the car and my mom was already at the front door waving us in.

My dad came trotting around the corner in his wolf form. I shook my head and called him out via our mind speak link. Dad. If you think you can intimidate my mate, think again. Remember, she's the one who smacked a one-blood on the nose and called him a bad dog.

I think that story, even more than the call from Selena, had changed my dad's mind about Charley. He liked anyone who stood up to one-bloods.

I know, my boy. But she's never met an alpha before. She might as well get the full feel of it right away, since she's going to be the matriarch of the pack someday.

Warmth spread across my chest. He had already accepted my mate if he was thinking of her future with the pack. I hadn't been sure he really would until now.

Charley took my hand and looked over at my dad's wolf. "Oh, is this your dog? Isn't he a handsome boy?"

Oh, Goddess.

She held out her hand like she was going to pet my dad and I almost died. Then she slapped her thigh and laughed hard. "I'm just kidding, Mr. Teagan. I figured out right away, you had to be the alpha Eli looks up to so much. Nice to meet you, I'm Charlize."

My mom joined us and put an arm around Charley. "I like her Eli. You picked a good one. Anyone who can give your father shit is a keeper in my book. Now come in the house, turkey is almost ready."

Charley and my mom headed to the kitchen and my dad shifted, threw on some pants my mom always kept by the door, and steered me toward his den. The sports channel was already on and we spent the next half hour talking about the teams and who we thought were going to the bowl games. But he seemed a little distracted, kept looking toward the kitchen. Maybe he was as eager for turkey and stuffing as I was. Mom didn't allow snacking on Thanksgiving, so we'd be nice and hungry for dinner.

On a commercial break, my dad muted the TV with the remote. "Eli, you know you don't have to play ball if you don't want to."

I just about spit out my drink. "I thought you wanted me to play pro for a few years before I come home."

He nodded slowly, but frowned at the same time. "Sure, that'd be great, but only if that's what you want, kid. You're a talented young man and you'll be a great alpha someday."

I didn't know what to say. Scouts were all over me and teams had come courting. I was just about ready to sign with an agent. Something had held me back from pulling that trigger, though. My dad had given me something to think about. I'd have to talk it out with Char. She always helped me figure what to do in a way no one else could.

He slapped me on the back in that way he had that always let me know he understood. "You two ready for the mating ritual tonight?"

I did not want to have a sex talk with my dad. Yuck. "Mostly. She's learned a lot from the other wolftresses at school, and Selena Troika's been like a mentor, but I'm not sure anyone is ready for their first time."

"No, I suppose not. I definitely wasn't ready for you mom and her wiley ways." He glanced toward the kitchen and his wolf rose up in the glow in his eyes. When they mated, wolves didn't necessarily get to choose their own mates. It was all political, but they fell in love. Disgustingly always thinking they were sneaky going off to screw around.

"Ew, dad. I do not want to hear about you and mom..." I made a barfing nose.

"Ah, but the way she glowed for me in the moonlight. It was like there was no one else in that sacred circle but her and me. You'll see, kid. You'll see."

I'd heard about this glowing for your mate thing, but my dad had never mentioned it before. Supposedly, it was something that happened for fated mates, but Charley and I had been too busy fucking like bunnies during the last two full moons to bother going outside in the moonlight. I wasn't sure I believed in such a fairy tale, but I also hadn't really believed in fated mates before I met her either. So anything was possible.

"Boys, dinner." My mom called us, but Charley stood at the door smelling like pumpkin pie and lust. I couldn't wait to eat her up.

We followed my parents to the backyard where we always set up the big wooden table so any pack members who wanted could join us for dinner. There were usually a few.

Not today, no. This wasn't a few. The entire damn pack was outside. When Charley and I walked out together, they clapped and cheered like we'd just won a game or something. They patted us on the back and shook my hand, and the wolftresses gave Charley kisses on the cheek.

I didn't know what to say, but Charley laughed. "Uh, I guess your family likes me."

"Yeah. I think so." We sat near the head of the table by my parents, and it took a minute for the rest of the pack to get settled at the tables that stretched halfway through the yard. When everyone was finally seated, my dad nodded at me.

I just stared at him until Charley elbowed me in the ribs. "He wants you to say grace."

Gulp. My dad always did that. He was the alpha. I grabbed Charley's hand under the table and bowed my head. "Today we give thanks to the Goddess of the moon, who blessed us with the ability to let our true natures roam free and gave us the gift of..."

I'd heard this prayer a thousand times, heard the ancient stories of a goddess who loved her people so much she came down from the stars and gave us the ability to shift into wolf form, be the hunters, warriors, protectors, and family we were meant to be. Never before today had I paid attention to the words.

I cleared my throat and squeezed Charley's hand. "Gave us the gift of her love. Join me today, my fellow pack, my family, my friends, in lifting our voices to her. For tonight we feast."

That's where the traditional prayer ended, but I added one more part because it's what was in my heart. "And tonight we find love. May you all be blessed with a true fated mate."

Every member of the pack lifted their faces to the sky and howled, a chorus of voices joining mine. Charley kissed me on the neck, right over the mark she'd given me on our first night together. Then she lifted her voice, but not in an average howl. No, she used her words and quietly howled into my ear, "I love you, too."

EPILOGUE

CHARLIZE

Standing in the forest, in nothing but a flimsy, sheer scrap of material, with a bunch of were-wolves, was straight out of a horror movie.

I love horror movies.

I wasn't as freaked out about this mating ritual as I thought I would be. His dad said some words, they all shifted and howled at the moon, and then most went off to do their business. I knew they were around, but it didn't matter. They'd given us the modicum of privacy I'd hoped for.

Once Eli and I were here in his pack's sacred circle, I forgot about anyone else. With the moon shining down on him, I could swear he was glowing, especially for me.

He took my hands in his and gave me the gentlest of kisses. "You look so beautiful. I hardly know how I got so lucky to have you for my mate."

Aww. While I loved his gentle kisses, I loved our passionate, can't-wait-to-tear-your-clothes-off ones even more. I grabbed Eli around the shoulders and pulled his head down to mine, and did my best to kiss the bejeezus out of him. Luckily for us both, there weren't a lot of clothes to tear off.

Eli was already naked, and I was liking the fact that wolf shifters burst out of their clothes when they took on their beast forms. That meant they were naked a lot. I wasn't sad about seeing my boyfriend, my lover, my love in his sexy glory at any time.

We dropped to the ground, and he tore the light bit of material right off me. "Char, I know I promised to tease you and do all kinds of naughty things to you tonight, but goddess, I need to be inside of you. I swear I'll do all those other things later."

"Funny, I was about to say the same thing to you." I reached out and stroked his cock, partly because I loved seeing his eyes roll back in his head when I touched him, and mostly because I couldn't wait any longer either. "This entire day has been one big tease. I've been ready for you since breakfast."

Eli grinned and growled, which was one of my favorite wolfy things he did. "I know. I could smell your arousal all day. Why do you think I had a napkin in my lap throughout dinner? It's not like I have great table manners."

That was true. Eli and his teammates didn't just eat, they massacred meals. "Why Eli Teagan, are you saying you've been this hard for me all day? You must have blue balls by now."

"You have no idea, my love." He grabbed my butt and gave it a squeeze. "On your hands and knees. I need to see this lush ass when I'm taking you tonight."

While I didn't always like the size of my butt, Eli was slightly obsessed with it. I got onto all fours and waggled it at him just because I knew it drove him wild. He was over me in a second, and I heard his harsh breathing. I loved it when he let go and lost a bit of his control.

"Say you're mine, Charlize. Say it." The words were snarled, and that made my heart go ka-thump.

Normally, I did exactly what he wanted because we both enjoyed this part of our sexy times. But tonight, I wanted more. "You're mine, you say it first."

That did it. That let Eli's beast out exactly like I wanted. When he let himself be free like this, I knew I had the real Eli, the one I loved so hard that I never wanted to let go. Every day, average Eli was sweet, and kind and I loved that side of him too, but I knew he had to try to be that way. This was his true nature.

He fisted my hair and pushed me closer to the ground, but with his other arm, he grabbed my hip, holding me up so my ass was angled just right. He teased me with the tip of his cock, notching it just inside my entrance. "Tell me you're mine."

"You say it first," I repeated.

With one long, hard stroke, he pushed himself fully inside of me, filling me up so good it took my breath away. We fit together so perfectly that I groaned. "More, Eli. Tell me you're mine, make me yours."

"Fuck, Char." He thrust in earnest, fast and hard, like he couldn't control himself. In this position, he hit all the best spots inside of me and it didn't take long before my body was pulsing and pounding, so close to orgasm. Eli was close too, and he leaned over me, chanting in my ear, "Mine, you're mine."

He tipped my head to the side and scraped his teeth across the tender skin between my neck and shoulder, in that sensitive spot along my collarbone. Zips and zings of pleasure zoomed through me when he did that. Tonight, it wasn't enough. I wanted more. I wanted everything from him.

"Give me all of you, Eli. I need the real you, I love you, and only you."

He paused for a moment, growled and then fucked me even faster and harder. "I am yours, Charlize, only yours, and you are mine."

He nipped at my earlobe and then pressed his mouth against that spot again. In another hard thrust, he bit down, sinking his fangs into me just as I opened my mouth to tell him what he wanted to hear. An orgasm like no other ripped through me and I screamed out the words. "I'm yours, Eli."

His cock pulsed inside of me as he came, and I felt the wolf's knot enlarge and lock us together. We collapsed onto the ground and Eli rolled so I was wrapped up in his arms instead of squished into the leaves and dirt underneath his enormous body.

We were both breathing hard, drifting in the glow of our bodies joined. With every breath he took, he whispered out that he was mine, over and over. Every time he said it, more warmth and tingles spread from the place he'd bitten me to run all up and down my skin.

I never wanted to leave his arms. "I love you, Eli, man or beast. I love you. You're mine and I'm yours, forever."

Those were the words his wolf needed to hear, and the knot faded, releasing us from its hold. My body gave one more little after quake of a shivering little orgasm and Eli chuckled. "You like the wolf's knot, don't you?"

"You know I do." I snuggled into him.

He kissed the spot where he'd bitten me and sent more tingles through me. "I hope you also like the new wolf's mark you have."

"Is that what you did? It felt amazing. I feel different now." It was as if a new hotter blood ran through my veins. I was down for being hotter for Eli.

"Different how?"

"Like my senses are heightened or something." I blinked to clear my vision. Then I sneezed. "Like there's more of me and more of you, and just more of everything."

Eli gave me a squeeze. "I'll always take more of you."

"Wait, umm, like for real, something is happening. My skin is all tingly and I don't think it's just because your made me come so hard I nearly exploded. What's happening?"

One minute I was in Eli's arms, feeling the afterglow of our lovemaking and mating, and the next I was wagging my tail.

My. Tail?

Eli?

Ack. His name did not come out of my mouth. It was like I was talking with my mind.

Eli smiled down at me and patted my head. "You're the prettiest wolftress I've ever seen." Then he scratched behind my ears, and I nearly fell over with pleasure. Oops, yep, I actually fell over.

Wolftress? Are you saying I'm a wolf right now? I said into Eli's head and tried to get up. Wolf legs were not like human legs. I was going to have to learn how to walk all over again.

Eli shifted into his wolf form and licked me right across the face, err, uh, snout. *Yep. You are. I'd heard some humans the Troikas mated got special powers, but I didn't know if it was true.*

You knew this was going to happen, and you didn't tell me? My tail started wagging again, so it was hard to hide that this was the coolest thing that ever happened to me.

Come on, let's go for a brief run and let you stretch your new form. Hopefully, you'll be able to shift back just as easily. Eli gave my side a shove with his nose and helped me back up to my feet.

Wait. Do we have to have sex for me to shift?

Eli trotted away, gave a howl to the moon, and winked at me. Guess we'll have to find out.

Need more Big Wolf on Campus?

Grab the next book in the series now: *Bad Boy Wolf*

A COCKY JOCK WOLF BONUS EPILOGUE

THE BIG GAME

It turns out, getting marked by a wolf shifter makes you super, duper, insanely, monstrously, horny.

Like, I already had a serious case of the hots for my boyfriend, because, well, have you seen him? As sexy-licious as he is, he's twice as sweet. I call him my burnt cinnamon roll. Tough and hard on the outside, ooey gooey and slightly spicy on the inside.

All that meant I couldn't keep my hands off him under normal circumstances. But then he had to go and sink his teeth into me, giving me wolfy superpowers while we were having mating ritual sex, and now I was hornier than a... horn dog? Horny toad? Horny as the entire horns section of the marching band?

Everyone knows band geeks are good in bed. Because one time, at band camp... Never mind.

I'll tell you the worst place to have the raging hot hormones for one's boyfriend, and that is on the icy cold metal stands of the Dire Wolves game against our biggest the rivals, the Crescent State Demons. What's even worse than that? Eli was playing like dog poo.

His head was not in the game, and I knew exactly where it was.

In my pants.

He was going to be really upset if the Dire Wolves lost this game because of him, and I didn't have any idea what to do about. But I knew who did.

The whistle blew and the scoreboard honked denoting half-time was upon us. The fans collectively groaned at our abysmal score, and I watched Eli throw his helmet halfway across the field in frustration. Seeing him that upset almost calmed my libido. Almost.

He was also hot as hell when he was all riled up. Who knew I'd find super competitive men so damn sexy?

The band and the cheerleaders made their way onto the field, and I pushed through the crowds vying for half-time beers to drown their sorrows in to find someplace quiet enough for a phone call. I'd been texting with Selena for the past fifteen minutes, and she told me she had the solution, but she wanted me to call her. Something about not having a paper trail?

Ever since our mating ritual yesterday, my senses were on super high alert. I could smell, see, taste, feel, hear, and did I mention smell, everything a thousand times better than before. That included people's emotions. So weird. I was also stronger than before I got wolfy powers. The benefit of which was how easy it was breaking and entering into locked doors, hallways, and locker rooms I wasn't supposed to access.

I followed my sensitive nose down into the bowels of

the stadium, using brand new reflexes to avoid being seen by anyone. Once I made it into a secluded hallway, I dialed Selena.

"Listen," she said. No hello, how are you, fine thanks, how're you. "I should have warned you that Eli would be on the hunt for days after your mating."

"On the hunt? I don't think he wants to shift and go hunting for white fluffy bunnies during halftime."

"Hunting you. You've been humping like rabbits, I'm sure. Which is all fine and fun, but you need to give him a challenge, a chase. Alphas love a good chase. Until you do, he won't be able to think about anything else."

Crap. How was I supposed to do that in the next thirty minutes?

"Oh, and trust me, Charley. Let him catch you at the very last moment. You can thank me later for setting you up to have the best orgasms of your life." Selena hung up and I shoved my phone back in my pocket.

Okay, I was a smart cookie. I had before me, a locker room I wasn't supposed to be in, a game of tag with my boyfriend, that ended in orgasms, all while he was in uniform, in the next thirty minutes. I bet Elizabeth Bennet never had to do this to have sex with Darcy.

Too bad for her.

ELI

Grr. There was no fucking way we were going to win this game and it was my god-damned fault.

I was practically bursting out of my skin with every snap, and I couldn't for the life of my concentrate. I had so much aggression running through my veins I literally growled at a linebacker who tried to tackle me. I think he peed his pants.

Why? Because my dick was hard, and my head wasn't in the game. It was back in bed with Charley. Back in the forest, running through the leaves and bushes with her. Back in the sacred circle, marking her, claiming, her and making her my mate. Mine.

The last thing I cared about was this football game. Which I should because I knew full well the scouts were here. Now I got to head into the locker room and get my ass reamed by coach for playing like a damn asshole.

I went to slam my helmet into the locker, but the equipment guy standing nearby snagged it before I could break anything else. Fast hands. Whatever.

I slumped down onto my seat and took a long deep breath, ready to snap off anyone's head who even deigned to talk to me about how bad the first half of the game went. Instead of sweaty locker room and sweatier football player smells, I got a delicious whiff of ripe cherries.

Charley cherry.

That wasn't possible. She'd just been on my mind so much that I was clearly now hallucinating. I was ready to give up my entire career to get a taste of her, right here, right now. Until coach started yelling at us like I knew he would. He wasn't one for histrionics, so his raised voice was one we'd all learned to pay attention too. And I wanted to, I swear I did.

But that scent.

Maybe it was on my clothes in my locker? I slowly and stealthily turned on the bench so coach wouldn't think I wasn't listening and scanned my stuff. No, my clothes did have the faint scent of her, but this was stronger, newer. With another whiff, I zeroed in on my helmet. Yeah, here it was, so hot and delicious I could have licked the fucking school logo off the side.

How was her scent on my helmet? I glared over at my fellow shifter teammates. These dickbags chose the wrong day to play a prank on me. I was on the verge of snarling at Kirill when I caught another whiff of Charley. My wolf rose up and my senses went animalistic.

Where was she? I needed to find her, right the fuck now.

I scanned the room to seek out her hiding place, but there was no one here but the team and our support staff. Coach certainly wasn't hiding her behind his back.

Although that's where the wafting of ripe Charley cherry was coming from.

The only thing behind coach was the guy in his Dire Wolves fan jersey and baseball cap pulled low, collecting our towels and shit. Hold up. The team's people had uniforms of their own. Polo shirts that designated them as staff, not fan jerseys.

I stood up, like I was stretching out my legs, and paced a couple steps one way and then a few more toward the towel guy. That was no guy. How the fuck hadn't I noticed all the curves in all the right places. The growl I'd been trying to hold in burst right out of my throat.

"You got something you want to say, Teagan?"

Shit. Busted. "Yeah, coach. I know exactly what I want and I'm going to do everything to get it."

From underneath that baseball cap, a face peeked up at me, with eyes that shined with the glow of Chincoteague purple sparkling like a beacon. Charley.

My Charley, in a room full of high testosterone athletes and shifters hopped up on competition and inspiration. What the fuck was she doing here and how was I going to get her out without anyone noticing?

Coach slapped me on the back. "That's the right attitude. The rest of you need to get your head in the same space for the second half."

The other players stood and cheered in that weird way we do when we're trying to psyche ourselves up. That gave me the opportunity to stalk Charley around the edges of the room. Every step closer I got to her, she'd push the towel cart a little farther away like she was zigzagging to avoid me. I circled back the other way and slipped into the mass of players bumping chests and grunting at each other.

I never lost sight of her for a moment, but she whipped her head around trying to find me. Now, I've got you, little sneak. She glanced at the door to the training room, over at me, and grinned.

When I emerged a few feet from the door, I expected to be able to reach out and grab her by the arm and haul her into my hold. I didn't have a plan with what to do with her after I caught her, but it didn't matter, because she wasn't there.

My wolf went crazy, pushing to get out, to track her, hunt her, capture her.

The door to the training room clicked and opened the tiniest of cracks. "Can't catch me, I'm the Gingerbread man, err, girl."

Coach's voice boomed through the room. "Ten minutes till we take back this game, boys. Let's do this."

Yes, let's do this indeed.

CHARLIZE

$\mathcal{H}$oly stinky testosterone, Batman. Boys were so gross. Why did they all smell so bad? If I ever had to sneak my way into a locker room for super-secret sneaky sexy times with Eli, I was sticking air fresheners up my nose.

This had better work.

I abandoned my smelly towel cart in favor of this dark room. It was the perfect hiding spot, where I also knew Eli could hunt me down easily. We only had a few minutes left before the game started again and it had taken me far longer to get his attention than I'd thought.

Once he caught my scent though, game over. I saw the second his wolf started hunting me. The mark on my neck went all tingly and so did my girly bits. Selena was right. This was fun.

The door cracked open wide enough for Eli to slip into the room, but he closed it behind him and did not turn on the lights. "Charrrrrleeeeey. Where are you hiding naughty girl?"

I slipped down behind the massage table since it was that or a vat of ice water. One thing I didn't want to do was cool either of our libidos down. I set the athletic tape I snagged, down onto the floor and gave it a shove so it rolled toward the far wall, hoping it would make Eli think that's where I was hiding.

He stepped on the roll with his toe, halting its progress. "Good try. Now come out so I can eat you up."

While that sounded like a great idea, I didn't think we'd played this hunting game quite long enough. I scurried toward the ice water tank on my hands and knees, but about ten inches away, Eli snagged me around the waist and hauled me up into the air.

"Gotcha." Within seconds he had me flat on my back on the massage table and crawled right up there with me. "You aren't supposed to be here, Charlize."

I didn't even get to tell him I full-well knew that and the plan because he attacked me with kisses. That's my favorite kind of attack. Partially because I can give as good as I get. Except this time, Eli didn't give me a chance.

He kissed me hard, pushed my head to the side and scraped his teeth across my shiny new mark, and then shoved the jersey up to expose my chest and belly. Three months ago, I'd have squealed and tried to get away from any man who even thought about looking at my stomach. With Eli, I didn't have to. He loved every part of my body just as much as I loved his.

"When we get home after the game, I'm going to fuck you good and hard, and spank this luscious ass for sneaking into my locker room on game day."

Hell, yeah. "Why not right now?"

He growled at me and nipped and bit his way across my chest, then down to my belly button. A centimeter from the waistband of my leggings, he grinned up at me with that glow in his eyes that made my insides go all squidgy. "Because I have approximately seven minutes before I have to be back out on that field. And while I know I could come in your hot cunt in that amount of time, you probably wouldn't get off that quick."

"I might." I was pretty damn turned on right now.

"I can smell your arousal, my sweet, but I know your body. You need more than my cock to make you come." In one fell swoop he had my leggings and panties down around my ankles, my knees spread, and his face buried between my thighs.

Just as he was licking his way up one side of my clit and down the other, someone knocked on the door. "Dude, hurry the fuck up. We're out here covering for you, so this better be what gets your head back in the game."

Eli didn't even pause for a second. Instead, he pushed two fingers inside of my channel and sucked on my clit so hard while finding just the right spot that I had to literally cover my own mouth not to howl out his name. With a few more strokes, some lashes of his tongue in all the best ways, and his thumb tickling the entrance to my ass, I came so hard I saw not just stars but a super nova.

He crawled up over me, gave me a quick bite on my mark and an even quicker kiss. Then he was gone, and I laid there for a long time trying to recover from the most epic orgasm I'd had since... well, last night. But it was certainly the fastest orgasm I'd ever had. Phew.

I laid there until I heard the stadium erupt into an explosion of cheers above me. The announcer shouted, "Touchdown Dire Wolves!"

I giggled so hard I almost fell off the massage table. That was my cue to pull my pants back up and get back to the game. Hopefully no one would notice I was walking funny. Nah, they wouldn't because the entire school would be focused on Eli leading the team to victory.

We won the game 35-17. I set a new school record for passing yards, and we secured our spot in the upcoming bowl season. The guys razzed me hard, but I overheard several of them plotting for how to sneak Charley into the locker room for our next game.

Charley didn't walk straight for a week after that. We both learned how much she liked being chased, caught, and spanked. I couldn't get enough of her. Fucking her, making her come, and telling her how in love with her I was.

While football was fun and gave me a lot of future prospects, none of it mattered to me as much as she did. No matter what we did in the future be it the NFL for me or having her own bookshop for Charley, I'd be happy and fulfilled if we were together.

Now if I could just get the rest of the shifters on the team mated.

"Sweetness, you got any friends at the Moon Bean that might be into football playing wolf shifters?"

Charley shrugged and gave me a sweet, sloppy smile. I couldn't ask for a whole lot more since I'd just made her come for the fourth time tonight. "I don't know, but I bet Selena does. She's always threatening one of us with getting fired if we don't go on dates."

"I think Kirill needs a girl." He was wound way too tight and needed to get laid.

Char made a face. "No, he needs an attitude adjustment."

"Fine, then how about Ty?" He was all up in my business all the time. If we got him a girlfriend or a mate, that would be good for my peace of mind.

"He doesn't need to be set up, he needs to get his head out of his ass and see what's right in front of him?" She rolled over and snuggled into me. Which of course had me going hard again.

"Luka?" He was working evenings at the Wolf's Den to help cover what his partial scholarship didn't. He could use a good time."

"Every girl likes a bad boy. Finding him a date will be easy. I'll tell Selena. She'll work her magic."

That was enough matchmaking for one night. Time to work my magic on my mate again and again and again.

Need more Big Wolf on Campus?

Grab the next book in the series now: *Bad Boy Wolf*

Chapter One
Hunter

I closed the book and sighed, holding the paperback to my chest. "God, I love a good happy ever after."

Yes, I did read the last page of the book first. I had to be sure I'd get the warm and fuzzies from the ending. Later, in the safety of my room, I'd flip through and read the naughty bits. Only then did I start at the beginning and read the whole story.

"Even better when it's got all the sexy times." Charlize slid the book out of my tightly clutched grasp and put it back on the shelf. "I don't see how you can read the endings of every book in the shop and skip the sex bits. That's half the fun of romance novels."

Heat rose up my throat and cheeks like I'd been drinking a glass of red wine, and I stared up at the ceiling hoping

Charlie wouldn't notice. I only blushed like this when I lied or had to get up in front of a class, or talk to people, especially guys. Okay, I blushed all the time and I hated it.

"Oh my God, you do read the sexy bits. Hunter, your followers would die if they found that out." Charlize laughed and pulled a bunch of other books off the shelf from the erotic romance section. She thrust them into my arms.

Like I didn't know that. My blog, Insta and TikTok, the Hunter of Hearts was dedicated to reading romance novels, but my whole platform was built on skipping the naughty bits. No smutty books allowed. Even if I coveted them and stalked other influencers pages for their recommendations. "Urrgh. I know. But so would my grandmother, my father, his new wife, and my older sister."

I sipped my mochaccino and flipped through the stack of new releases Charlie had chosen for me and handed them all back. I'd already read every single one of them, some two or three times. But on my super-secret sneaky Amazon account that loaded to my Kindle where no one could see what I was reading. "It's too late now. I can't come out of the romance reading closet and be like 'Hey, everyone, I like to read super dirty books to get my jollies. Sorry for making you think I was a good girl."

My favorite coffee shop across from campus, the Moon Bean, recently expanded their business and added a bookshop that stocked everyone's favorite genre literature. I spent more time and money here than anyone reasonably should. But, come on. Two of my favorite guilty pleasures under one roof? What more could a lonely, horny girl with a goody-two-shoes reputation to protect ask for?

Selena, the owner, grabbed a copy of Maya Rodale's *Dangerous Books for Girls: The Bad Reputation of Romance Novels Explained* and handed it to me. "Hey, no literary snobbism allowed here. You can read whatever you want, whenever you want, for whatever reason you want. Just as long as you read."

"Tell that to my grandmother. She's already made it perfectly clear that majoring in contemporary literature is her worst nightmare. Unless of course it's just a stepping stone for law school or I get on at a Big Five publisher as an acquiring editor, which she is sure to make happen." I tucked the book into my stack of purchases for the day even though I already owned a copy. I'd give it away on my next TikTok live event. The booktok community went crazy for giveaways.

"Hunter, you need to relax, you're stressing me out and I can't write when you're freaking out." Rosemary, the resident creative writing major, who didn't want anyone to know she was writing a romance novel, shouted from her spot in the corner of the coffee shop. She was the only girl I knew who drank more coffee than me. I liked her and couldn't wait to read her book. It was sure to have all the naughty bits I craved in it.

Selena smiled and patted me on the back. "Don't listen to her, she won't even admit what she's writing about to the person who needs to know."

"Ooh, who needs to know?" Perfect opportunity to change the subject.

"Good try." She gave me a smirk. But you should listen to me. You need to relax."

The way she said relax, with the ah-sound all drawn out and with an eyebrow waggle indicated she meant more than getting a massage or taking a bubble bath. And there went the heat rising up my cheeks again.

Charlize blinked and held up a finger. "Isn't that what Rosemary just said?"

"Shoo. Go stock the new horror books we just got in. Your handsy quarterback boyfriend is reading me out of house and home." Selena made the go-away motion to Charlize and then propped herself against the shelf next to me.

"What you need is to go on a date and get some of this nervous energy out of your system." She wagged her finger up and down pointing from my toes to my head and back again.

"A date?" Yeah, that was my voice that sounded like Minnie Mouse. I cleared my throat. "I don't see how that's going to relax me even a little."

"Hmm." Selena examined me like I was some kind of book display that needed re-arranging. "No, you're right. Just any old date won't do for you. You're too wound up about the whole thing. What you need are some good old-fashioned dating lessons."

How did she know I knew less than nothing about dating and boys? Not nothing, I knew what book boyfriends were like. I was also smart enough to know that real life guys were nothing like romance heroes. "You're going to teach me how to find a boyfriend?"

"Oh-ho-ho. No. The best person for that job is a big

flirt with charm to spare, so he can lend a little to you." She tapped her finger on her lips. Selena was this super gorgeous, mature, curvy woman who was more charming than anyone I knew and flirted with ninety percent of the professors and other older men who came into the shop. If not her, then who?

Wait. Did she say he? Ack. No. I clammed up like a bonfire at the Cape if a cute guy even looked at me. Which they rarely did. College guys did not make passes at girls in glasses with big... well, you know. Let's just say, I was no Victoria's Secret model. I knew it. Guys knew it. End of story.

"I've got it. Pack up your bags, we're going next door." Selena shoved the books I wasn't going to buy into a bag and handed it to me.

"To The Wolves' Den? I don't think anyone there would to want to give me dating and flirting lessons." That place was notorious for hook-ups. Especially with the Dire Wolves players. The football team was too sexy for their shirts and not looking to find the love of their lives. Except maybe Charlie's boyfriend, Eli.

Those two were in mega love.

"Ah, you're wrong there. I know just the bad boy whose flirter is a well-oiled machine." Selena didn't wait for me to make my purchases or anything. She shoved my backpack onto my shoulder and led me by the arm out the door of the Moon Bean and down the sidewalk.

"No, Selena, please. I don't think this is a good idea. It's fine. I'm fine." Not only were my cheeks heating up, so was my throat and chest. Then there was ka-thumping in my chest like my heart was in an Edgar Allan Poe story. I might be fine putting myself on camera for my followers, but that was because I could use filters, and ring lights, and just the right angles to look good. In real life, I'd be practically bare.

Better to stick to book boyfriends. Or, uh battery operated ones. Or both at the same time.

Selena wrapped her arm around my shoulder and gave me a friendly squeeze. She treated all of regulars who hung out at her shop like an adopted family of sorts. I certainly felt more affection and care from her than my own grandmother or any of my string of stepmothers. "I'm doing this for your own good. Get your butt in that bar and learn to loosen up around the fellas, or you're fired."

"What? Wait. I don't work for you." My father insisted it was improper for me to work while studying. There would be plenty of time for that after I graduated. The only work I did was on my website and socials, and I'd been forbidden to monetize any of that, so it's not like it paid in anything but fans and books. I didn't need the money anyway.

"You're right, but you do use The Moon Bean to write your blog and get the latest and greatest romance novels. So, unless you go in there and get your flirt on, I'm banning you from the shop."

I gasped. "You can't do that."

Could I work on my hobby at home? Yes. Did I love being around other people who lived the book nerd life like me? Also yes, and having my own place off campus was boring and lonely. I'd go crazy if I didn't get to hang out at the Moon Bean.

"Of course I can. Now get in there." She yanked open the door to The Wolves' Den and shoved me inside the bar.

The stench of beer and bodies hit me first. I wasn't used to spending time in college dive bars, even though I was in college. This place was for rowdy beer-drinkers and risky shot-takers. That was so not me. I was more of a champagne bubbles tickle my nose kind of girl.

The second thing that hit me was the chest and six-pack abs of the guy I walked smack into while gawking at my surroundings and feeling out of place.

"Whoa, hey there. Walk much, sweetheart?" He grabbed me by the arms and kept me from falling right on my butt.

Once I got my balance, I looked up into the sexiest eyes I'd ever seen. They sparkled and everything, just like in the romance novels. Then he winked. Oh my God, he winked at me and my lady parts went haywire.

I blame them for what came out of my mouth next. Because never in my life had I ever said something so insane to anyone, ever.

"Will you teach me how to flirt?"

End of Sample

To continue reading, be sure to pick up _Bad Boy Wolf_ at your favorite retailer.

BOOKS BY AIDY AWARD

ALPHA WOLVES WANT CURVES

In a world where the Wolf Tzar rules, pack politics decides one's fate, and matchmaking matriarchs know what's best, it shouldn't be this hard for a son of the most powerful pack on the East Coast to get a date. But when the forces of good and evil are battling to decide who these heroes can take as a mate, revolution is in the air. Who knew one little assassination and the chance to be with their true fated mates could change the wolf-shifter world forever?

DRAGONS LOVE CURVES

In a world of curvy witches, flower nymphs, masquerade balls, and succubi, it shouldn't be this hard for a dragon to find his mate. But when the forces of good and evil are battling for your soul, romance has to wait. Unless the First Dragon and the Goddess of Love insist on matchmaking.

BLACK DRAGON BROTHERHOOD

Spin-Off of Dragons Love Curves

Fated Mates. Forbidden Love. A Battle Against Hell Itself.

The Black Dragon Brotherhood was forged in fire and blood—an elite force of dragon shifters sworn to protect the world from darkness. But when the rise of shadow demons threatens to consume everything in its path, these powerful warriors must risk more than their lives to stop them. Their greatest weapons? The curvy, brilliant, and dangerously irresistible women they never saw coming.

BIG WOLF ON CAMPUS

What do young, athletic wolf shifters do when they're in their prime? Go play football for Bay State University Dire Wolves! Oh... and they just might fall in love and find their fated mates, with a little help from a meddling matriarch of one of the most powerful wolf families in the world.

VAMPIRES CRAVE CURVES

They're deadly spies, immortal warriors, and ruthless protectors of the night. But when it comes to their fated mates… even vampires have a sweet tooth.

The Vampire Intelligence Agency operates in the shadows, ensuring that the Immortal Royals remain safe and that humans never discover the truth about what lurks in the dark. These elite operatives—master spies, lethal assassins, and brilliant strategists—are the best at what they do. They never fail a mission. Until fate throws them a mission they never expected—love.

STANDALONE

Claimed by the Winter Realm

ABOUT THE AUTHOR

Aidy Award is a curvy girl who kind of has a thing for stormtroopers and shifters. She writes curvy girl romance, about real love, and dirty fun, with happy ever afters because every woman deserves great sex and even better romance, no matter her size, shape, or what the scale says.

Read the delicious tales of hot heroes and curvy heroines come to life under the covers and between the pages of Aidy's books. Then let her know because she really does want to hear from her readers.

Connect with Aidy on her website www.Aidy-Award.com, sign up to get her Curvy Connection emails, and join her Facebook Group - Aidy's Amazeballs.

Aidy also writes curvy girl sports romances as Amy Award. If that's your jam, check those books out at authoramyaward.com.

amazon.com/Aidy-Award/e/B00KP8DNVU

patreon.com/AidyAward

bookbub.com/authors/aidy-award

goodreads.com/aidyaward

tiktok.com/@aidyawardbooks

facebook.com/aidyaward

instagram.com/aidyaward

ABOUT PIPER FOX

Piper Fox writes short steamy paranormal romances for sassy, strong-willed women who love sexy alpha men, fated mates, and insta-love. When she's not writing... oh, who is she kidding, she's always writing or reading in her favorite genres - paranormal and sci-fi romance.

Join her on Facebook for of hot heroes pics, book nerd memes and other foxy fun! facebook.com/PiperFoxAu thor

facebook.com/PiperFoxAuthor
bookbub.com/profile/piper-fox
amazon.com/Piper-Fox/e/B08954Y89V

ACKNOWLEDGMENTS

It's always great to have writing friends to do projects with! Piper and Aidy would like to thank M. Guida, McKenzie Rogue, Michelle Ziegler, and Candice Bundy for being great friends and we're both looking forward to more retreats and projects together with you!

Readers - if you haven't checked out any of these authors, we think you'll love each and every one of them!

From Aidy:

I am so very grateful to my Patreon Book Dragons!

Shout out to my Official VIP Fans!

Thank you so much for all your undying devotion for me and the characters I write. You keep me writing (almost) every day.

Extra Hugs to you ~

- Angie K.
- Anna Marie P.
- Barbara B.
- Corinne A.
- Jeanette M.
- Elisha B.

- Kerrie M.
- Natasha H.
- Orma M.
- Sandra B.
- Sara W.
- Tracy L.
- Zoe W.
- Frania G.

And enormous thanks to my Official Biggest Fans Ever. You're the best book dragons a curvy girl author could ask for~

Hugs and Kisses and Signed Books for you from me!

- Alida H.
- Cherie S.
- Dale W.
- Danielle T.
- Daphine G.
- Jessica W.
- Katherine M.
- Kelli W.
- Marilyn C.
- Mari G.
- Melissa L.
- Rosa D.
- Stephanie F.
- Stephanie H.